The Saga Of Ukumog

Wracked
Desecrated

Threads of Ukumog

Shadow of the Pyramid

SHADOW OF THE PYRAMID

By Louis Puster III

Sean,

Are you sure it is safe here?

Scared,
Louis Puster III

This is a work of fiction. All the characters and events portrayed in this book are either products of the author's imagination or are used fictitiously.

SHADOW OF THE PYRAMID

Copyright © 2014 by Louis Puster III

All rights reserved, including the right to reproduce this book, or portions thereof, in any form.

Edited by Morgan A. McLaughlin McFarland
Cover Art by Chandler Kennedy & Louis Puster III

First Edition
ISBN 1500874647
ISBN 978-1500874643

For Bruce

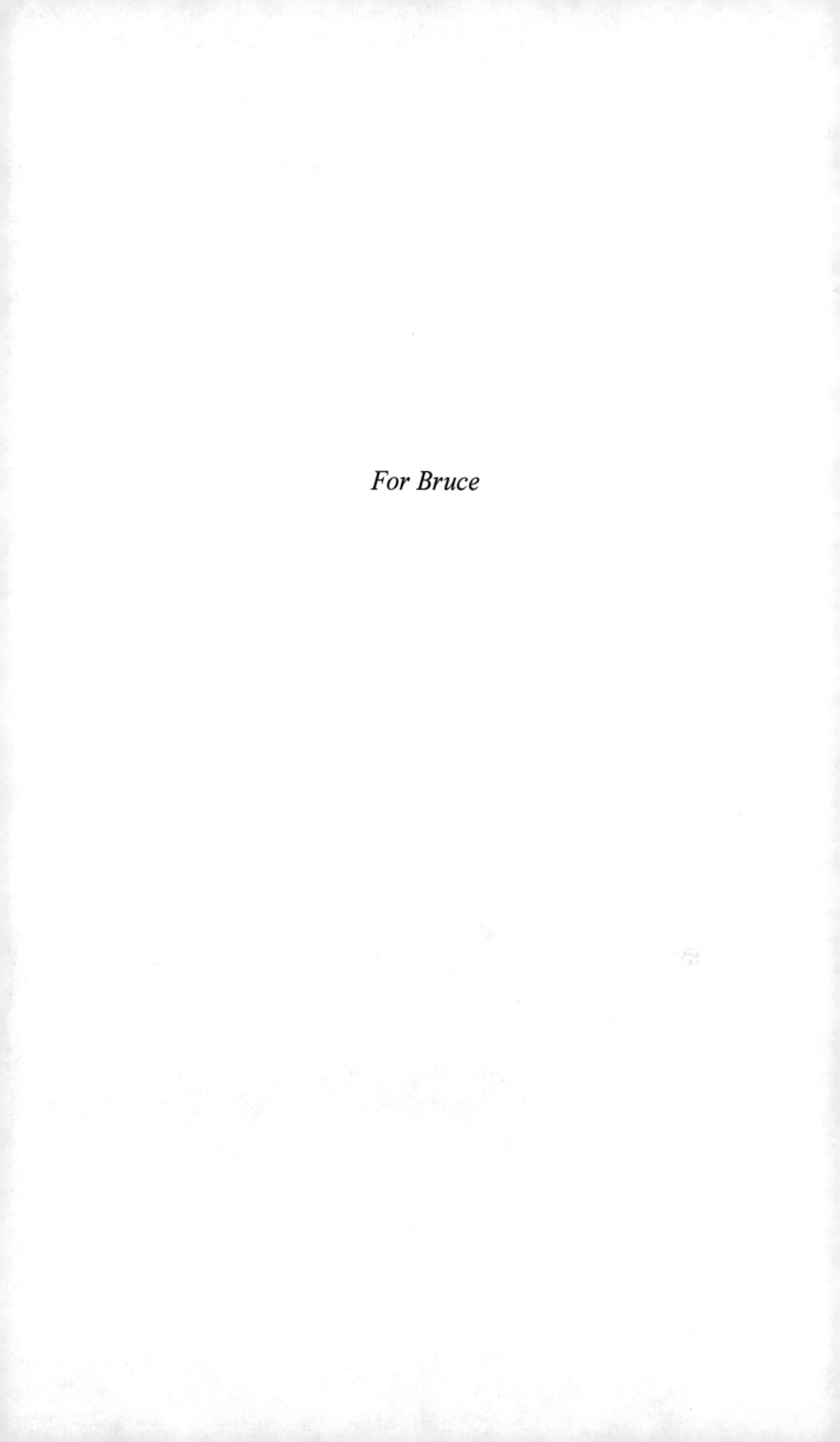

Chapter 1

At first, the hard soapy bristles of the brushes stung his flesh as they scratched their way over his tough skin. Maybe it was the repetitive motion of the brushes in the hands of the trained acolytes that changed it from scraping to soothing, or maybe it was the hypnotic mixture of the incense in the room and the drugs in his blood. Either way, it didn't matter to Moriv. The pain became pleasure and put him into a trance. His life prior to being here in this dark chamber had been full of nothing but toil. As a slave, there was no time for any joy. The pleasure in this bath was a whispered myth among the other slaves. Two days before he found himself here, Moriv's life was changed.

In the shadow of the Great Obsidian Pyramid there lay the city of Shatter. The denizens of the city lived there, always protected from the searing rays of the sun. There were many types of people who lived in Shatter. Most of them, however, were slaves. Each person owed their existence to the Great Obsidian Pyramid, and so everyone in Shatter was a follower of the Mari'Andi, those who spoke of the secrets within the stone. Everyone in Shatter worshiped the Pyramid for all it had done, and all it would someday do for them. It was their divine lord.

Shadow of the Pyramid

The day on which Moriv's life was changed was a holy day. Most of the city was gathered in the Obsidian Plaza which lay at the feet of the Great Pyramid. The black stone of the plaza gleamed darkly in the light that was present on that day. Moriv, before he was Moriv, found himself kneeling in a sea of slaves near the back of the plaza. The lines carved into the plaza made sections which determined how close to the Pyramid a person was allowed to be. Common slaves like Moriv, being the most unworthy, were all the way in the back of the plaza. Chimes and chanting from the priests on the dais where the Pyramid itself rested drifted out over the assembled crowd. From where the man who would become Moriv huddled, he could barely hear them. There was a certain amount of excitement in the crowd that day. News that the priests had been given a divine vision had already permeated the layers of Shatter. Everyone, even the slaves, expected something special.

First came the normal parade of priests all dressed in fine black silks with silver chains tied around their waists. The more important priests had nine-tail whips with shards of obsidian looped into their length. Still more of them came. The next priests wore faceless black masks decorated with glinting silver veins slithering through them. On this particular holiday, slaves of the Pyramid's temple carried large fragments of the Pyramid through with the priests. The slave that would be Moriv always tried to imagine where the individual pieces fit into the colossal cracked structure that they all worshiped. He had even heard one slave—one that was shortly thereafter never seen from again—say that the temple itself was held together by the lingering shadows of the ancient lords of Shatter. In those deep places, all the history of the world could be seen, but none except the Scion of the temple could weather the

Chapter 1

storm of secrets. Still, the slave who would become Moriv could not help but wonder how his divine master had suffered the wounds in its massive stone form.

"Keep your head down, slave!" Then followed the expected crack of a leather club on the slave Moriv's back. He had been staring again, and it was only his place to worship, not to look.

The procession that day was twice or three times as long as the normal ones. Many of the powerful guilds from Shatter made their presence known with some theatrical display. Unfortunately, Moriv the slave had his face to the ground, and could only feel the heat of the fire as the entertainers went past, or see distorted ghosts of their likeness reflected in the patterned obsidian mirror upon which he knelt. He dare not look up again, else face more beating.

Next to last to go up the wide aisle of the plaza that day was a slave-pulled chariot. Each of the slaves was tied to the chariot with barbed silver chains, their eyes replaced with carven images crafted out of the darkest obsidian. These slaves were the property of the High Priest of the Mari'Andi, Konrix, and they must pay with blood for their direct contact with the Pyramid itself. It is an honor to serve the Mari'Andi and therefore the suffering of those who are unworthy is never ending. Konrix stood atop the chariot, which was drenched in silks and velvet. On the tier below him lounged the circle of his concubines, each of them tempting every slave to look up at them.

As the chariot rode past, Moriv could hear the dying screams of those slaves who dared to look upon the glory of Konrix or lust after his harem. Their deaths would not be a waste, as the slave knew. Their blood would be used to glorify the Great Obsidian Pyramid, and any souls sacrificed in the plaza would be absorbed into its bosom. He had been given the duty once of cleaning up the bodies of those who had willingly offered their lives in the plaza after a day of faith. The bravery of those that silently bleed themselves dry in the plaza amidst the crowd was something he could not help but respect.

"Brothers and sisters! May you always walk in darkness!" Konrix's voice bellowed out over the crowd. "Our Scion has returned from the light to us. Praise be to the almighty Pyramid! Praise be to the ancestors!"

"Praise be to the almighty! Praise be to the ancients!" the crowd responded in complete unison. The slave who would be Moriv was no exception.

One last cart rumbled down the aisle. Surprised by this unusual addition, the slave had to try and catch a glimpse. Through the kneeling bodies that surrounded him, he could just barely make out white silk robes, partially soaked in the blood of the slaves who wore them. As the cart shook the stone and passed by, he caught glimpses of white wheels with images of Pyramids carved into the creamy surface of the cart, and then it was out of view. The temptation to lift his head was burning within him, but the fear of displeasing his master was greater, that is, until he heard the gasps and applause from the sections where those who were allowed to look knelt. Grinding his teeth together and tapping his forehead to the ground, he was able to resist the temptation.

Nearby, one of the plaza pacifiers sensed the energy of this one unruly slave, and started heading over to where he knelt. The leather club in the pacifier's hand creaked with glee at the prospect of reminding the slave of his place. The pacifier crept slowly up on the disrespecting filth. As he drew closer, he held his breath to steel his body in preparation of the righteousness he was about to deliver. Though he had done this countless times, each chance to give praise to the Great Pyramid by doing his duty made him excited and nervous. That, and he really enjoyed it.

Chapter 1

The Moriv slave's curious compulsion to lift his head and gaze upon the pristine shape of the Scion was a battle he could not win. He knew without a doubt that there would be consequences, but he could not help himself. He lifted his head.

Flowing white silks trailed the cart. They were so thin that the lightest breeze made by the cart's movement caused them to dance behind it. The sides of the cart were high and latticed with ivory windows, but the back and top remained open. Inside, soft shining folds in lush velvet made a thick bed for the man who was sleeping deep within. Slave Moriv had never had a bed, nor had he ever even heard whisper of a bed that lush. Briefly, he imagined himself swallowed in that silk and velvet, embraced by the cool comfort of the soft fabrics within that cart.

Whack!

Pain did not come at first. The leather clubs of the pacifiers were designed to deliver long lasting pain that would not cause unnecessary damage to those they 'pacified'. By the time slave Moriv figured out what had happened, the second the third blows had come down on his head and back.

"Face to the ground. You are unworthy. Face to the ground!" the pacifier shouted.

Moriv tried to comply with the pacifier's will, but even after he was huddled to the ground with his forehead touching it, the beating still came. By then, the pain from the first blow had started to throb through him, and the rest were in line to show the club's belligerent affection for Moriv's actions.

The cracking of this particular club on this particular slave seemed no different than the other five slaves being beaten at that very moment. Furthermore, the pacifier had beaten at least thirteen other slaves on this very day for various offenses. After all, he was just doing his duty, and slaves tend to misbehave from time to time. Something about this beating, however, was not normal.

A voice called out, and the white ivory cart stopped moving on the gleaming obsidian plaza. "Stop. Stop beating that slave."

At first, the pacifier didn't hear the voice and continued his work, but when the silence of the entire plaza was filled with only the sounds of his particular club, he realized his mistake. With hesitation, he looked up and found the gaze of the Scion upon him. There stood the Scion, wrapped in white silk, fiercely staring at the pacifier. Anxiety filled the crowd. From on the dais, Kronix looked on confused and uncertain as to what would happen next. Each Scion had been different. They live outside the rules. Being declared the direct child of the ancestors who bring power and life to the Pyramid - they are like living gods. Konrix knew that this Scion's time was ending, but he had not been given instruction as to exactly what was about to happen. As high priest of the Mari'Andi, he had seen many Scions come and go, but this time something was different.

"I said stop. You will not beat him anymore." The Scion spoke with soft yet thunderous words.

The pacifier fell to the ground. His palms slapping the obsidian, ringing out like two cracks from his leather club. "Forgive me, Master. He was trying to look upon you. It is forbidden—"

"Not forbidden to this one."

"But, he is a slave, Master. Just a slave."

"And I was once a slave. Were you not one once? All of us here in Shatter must spend time as a slave. It is what makes us unlike the rest of the world. Outsiders are soft. Their hands are soft, their hearts, their minds. But we are not soft." He paused for a moment and locked eyes with Moriv. The muscles in The Scion's

Chapter 1

face became slack, and his eyes opened wide. Slowly he approached the place where Moriv lay in a ball on the ground. "We are the dagger that will drive death into the heart of the Betrayer for once and for always. The Maze did not work. The Prison did not work. Nor has the Tomb. These little slumbers have proven nothing. It is up to us."

Moriv lifted his face to the Scion, and for a moment it seemed that the halo of the sun's rays, which had always been around the edge of the Pyramid, shone around the edges of the Scion's bald head. The pain of the pacifier's club was beginning to fade, replaced by confusion. From somewhere in the flowing silk, the Scion's hand appeared and reached towards Moriv. Instinctively, he reached out for it. When the two hands met, audible gasps erupted from the masses. The Scion pulled Moriv to his feet and proclaimed to the entire assembly, "I give you Moriv, the next Scion."

With no hesitation, the fanatical crowd erupted with frenzied cheering. As he rode with the white clad Scion to the dais, he realized what was happening. Moriv was no longer a nameless slave. Now, everything was different. Moriv was silent as he approached the Great Pyramid. He felt an awe unlike any other, as if the ancients were looking back at him from the shattered surface.

They disembarked from the white chariot, and servants of the Great Pyramid rushed forward and tore the rags from Moriv's body. Others came rushing to him with cleansing oils and linen towels. They washed his chest and back and then wiped him dry. Konrix came and stood at Moriv's left side, and the previous Scion stood at his right. The crowd moved up and down like waves of the ocean flowing in Moriv's direction, but Moriv had never seen the ocean.

Shadow of the Pyramid

Two red hot brands were brought to the front of the dias. Each of the brands held the mark of the Great Pyramid, a triangle with an eye in the center. The Scion took the first brand and stepped behind Moriv, who knew what was about to happen.

"Behold! I am the past. Know me and my trials. Let our history become part of you. I give you my path!" With these ritual words, the Scion pressed the brand against Moriv's back. The pain of the brand was greater than any pain he had ever felt before. Then the Scion took hold of the sharp end which lay opposite the brand and aimed it at his heart. Step over step, he drove himself onto the spike at the other end of the brand, driving the sharp metal into his chest. When the Scion could no longer press himself forward, slaves of the Pyramid helped press him until he stood directly behind Moriv, his white silk robes soaked in blood and caught fire in the heat of the brand. Other slaves came swiftly with blankets to put out the fire, then retreated from the ceremony.

"I am the future," Konrix called out as he took the other brand and stepped in front of Moriv. "Come and make the path of our people yours." Konrix stood with the brand outstretched towards Moriv.

Moriv could not see the crowd or hear their cheers anymore. The pain from the first brand had placed him in a haze where all he could see was Konrix and the brand before him. He knew what he must do, but it took him time to get his legs to respond. Finally, he took one step, then another. Cool air filled the space between his back and the brand he left behind, and the pain of the burns shot through his body. Still he struggled towards Konrix.

Chapter 1

Smoke hissed from the brand as soon as Moriv's chest made contact. Unable to hold back any longer, he screamed with fury at the pain that now embraced his whole torso. Konrix looked on with approval. He knew that the now-dead Scion had chosen with divine insight.

After the brand had done its work, Konrix removed it from Moriv's chest and threw it to the marble floor of the dais. He took Moriv's hand and raised it along with his own in celebration to the crowd. Howling madness from the crowd filled the sky, and Moriv's vision faded to darkness.

When he awoke, Moriv found himself in a small chamber. The walls and floor were made of obsidian and were decorated only with the many cracks which snaked through the shining stones like veins. As his eyes traced the lines of the cracks, he realized that he was within the Great Pyramid itself.

His bed was a lush pit of silks and velvets. The softness of the fabric was like touching pure joy, or at least as much joy as he had ever known. He could not help but gently rub each of the textures against his face. A smile found its way to his face, and it, too, was something he had barely known. The simple pleasures of a comfortable life made it seem like he was caught in a dream, but the cost of such pleasures had not yet come to him.

His torso hurt, but slaves learn to ignore the pain of their work. Wrapped around his body were bandages, holding herbs against his burns. While he had no memory of how the wrappings got there, he paid their appearance only a small moment of attention. Once aware of them, however, he did his best to not disturb them.

Every way he tried to lie on his soft bed gave him discomfort. Eventually he found himself sitting upright with his legs crossed. The stress of the pain made him very sleepy, and he

Shadow of the Pyramid

kept nodding off. His trust of the Pyramid slaves was unwavering. He knew that someone would come for him when the time was right, and come to him they did. When it was time to feed him, they did so, never letting his hand touch a utensil. When it was time to empty his chamberpot, they did so, waving powerful incense as they traveled. When it was time to change his bandages, they did so, taking delicate care of the throbbing wounds beneath. When it was time for sleep, the women came to see to his primal needs. Moriv had never mated with a woman before. Slaves were not allowed to spread their seed, but as Scion of the Great Pyramid it was expected.

    Countless days went on this way, and Moriv did not leave his room. In his dreams, he saw images of the old Scion, and he saw the world outside of Shatter. Most of his dreams did not make any sense, yet they troubled him. As the final days of his healing came, he started dreaming of a walled city filled with despair. Deep in the bowels of the city lived a regal lord that fed on the people above as a gluttonous shepherd feeds on his flock. In the darkness of that lord's chambers a blinding light came. A light which came from a dark blade. The regal lord fought against the villain who wielded the blade, but there was no hope. The light was too bright and cast away the shadows which protected the lord. The dark blade drank deep of the regal lord's blood and he was destroyed.

    Then there was nothing but hurried travel. Hills, valleys, plains, and mountains all flew by as the desperate flight stretched on. The panic which set this flight in motion came to an end the moment the horizon gave way to reveal a great black pyramid in the distance, and once he was within the shadow of it - there was peace.

Chapter 1

Moriv did not know what to make of these dreams, but he knew that they were meaningful. He tried to commit the feelings of the dreams to memory, so that he could recall them again when the time was right.

When the his healing was complete, the slaves took him for his cleansing, for soon he would be brought into the holiest chamber in the Great Pyramid - the Chamber of Ancient Thrones. The cleansing took place under the skilled hands of acolytes of the Pyramid. Their hard bristle brushes scraped away the dirt of Moriv's previous life. To ease the discomfort of the experience, Moriv was given herbs to chew which would strengthen him and cause him to reflect on how he go there in the first place.

So there he was, cleaner than he had ever known possible and being dried by the gentle hands of slaves. "No such luxury can come without price," he thought to himself. His mind drifted back to the sacrifice of the previous Scion, but to give one's blood for the glory of the Pyramid was no sacrifice at all. Then he remembered what Konrix had said when he announced the previous Scion, that he had traveled outside the protective shadow of the Pyramid. Moriv's mind sobered at just the thought of the outside world. As a slave, he had heard the terrible stories about life outside of the shadow. Would he now have to embrace such a life? The thought terrified him.

Moriv was so distracted that he hadn't noticed that the acolytes had finished drying him and anointing him with oils. Further, he didn't notice as they began to sew his new clothes around him, like a team of caterpillars weaving a cocoon for their king. Moriv didn't notice these things because his mind was reeling at the thoughts of what his future would hold. He was both terrified and exhilarated at the idea of the great and dangerous world beyond the Pyramid. As his intoxicated thoughts spun, he found himself the conqueror of far away nations, the ruler of unenlightened kingdoms, the savior of many fine women, a man who was in charge of his own destiny. Even with the drugs pumping through his system, he became infatuated with his own future and the potential therein.

Hours ticked by as the acolytes did their work. Moriv's unspoken thoughts of a heroic and depraved future caused time to fly by, and he was still drunk on his own potential when the silent acolytes began urging him to walk through the cracked obsidian hallways of the Pyramid. Every person whose path they crossed would avert their eyes and step out of the way of the box of acolytes that surrounded the white silk–clad Moriv.

The hallways grew in height and width as they came closer to the heart of the Great Pyramid, and very quickly they approached massive black doors trimmed in carved silver. The hinges of the doors barely made a sound as they opened on their own. Without hesitating, the box of acolytes around Moriv walked forward, but then, in practiced unison, the front split away before they crossed the threshold of the doorway. As the ranks of servants melted away, they formed a line at the door, which gave Moriv no choice but to follow his momentum into the room.

The walls of the room were slanted, not unlike the Pyramid which surrounded the room. The center of the room was open and filled with a strangely warm purple light. Standing in the center, looking up at the blinding source of light on the ceiling, was Konrix, the high priest of the Mari'Andi. Without knowing how, Moriv knew that Konrix was conversing with something unseen, and Moriv was strangely comfortable with it.

"Ah," Konrix shook off the unheard conversation and looked over at Moriv. "It is good that you have come, Scion. The ancestors and I have been thinking of you. We believe that it is time

Chapter 1

for you to know your quest. It will not be an easy one, make no mistake about that. Still, you are the one who has been chosen, and so you are the one who will take up the burden - for all of Shatter."

Moriv's mind was still taking in all the glistening shapes in the room. While the room itself was in the shape of the Pyramid in which it resided, it had raised rings in the floor, at different levels. All of the horizontal space on these different platforms were covered in chairs, thrones, stools, and other seats, each of them of the finest quality craftsmanship and draped in riches, but also bearing the marks of usage.

Konrix became aware of Moriv's awe struck stare regarding the host of seats and a smile came to the priest's face. "These are the thrones of the ancestors." Konrix grandly motioned toward them. "This is their final resting place. Here they become one with the Pyramid and whisper to us from beyond the grave."

At the slightest suggestion that he might be able to hear the whispers of the ancestors, Moriv opened his mind to the possibility. The caution that a life as a slave had taught him was now gone. Perhaps it was the days of pleasurable solitude, the drugs and incense that pulsed through him, or the realization that he was now above even Konrix in social standing that had wiped his fear away. Whatever the reason, he was awash with potential and power. Moriv stared at each of the thrones, searching them for some new experience. When his eyes fell upon a simple chair made of dark wood somewhat hidden behind the others, he felt something touch his mind.

"Hello child," came the raspy voice of an old man. "Now you will see."

Konrix saw fear take hold of Moriv's face, and the young Scion's body stiffened. Moriv stood—shaking violently, but unable to move—in the center of the room. His mind was under attack

Shadow of the Pyramid

from within. For the briefest of moments, Konrix was concerned, but then the ancients whispered to him not to worry. And so, Konrix waited.

Inside Moriv's mind, he saw a terrible scene. The Great Pyramid bled streams of light from its many cracks. These streams of energy grew more and more intense until finally the Pyramid exploded, sending fragments of obsidian in every direction. The debris fell upon the city of Shatter, pieces both big and small striking slaves and citizens alike with such force that they were killed instantly. Rooftops were caved in by showers of glistening dark stone. Burning rays of light overpowered the city and tormented the people caught outside. Chaos and calamity had come to Shatter, and these forces would not leave until everything had been destroyed. Without the Pyramid, there was no hope, no salvation from the painful rays of the sun, no peace in the structure of daily life. All would fall into ruin.

When the light from the explosion faded, a dark form stood in the crater where the Great Pyramid once stood. The form seemed completely made out of shifting shadows save for one thing: a glowing sword clutched in the shadow's grasp. The sword had a handle of bone wrapped with red leather, and its blade was as black as the shadow that held it. Upon the rectangle shape of the blade, however, were glowing runes which gleamed with blinding anger. Moriv knew that this horrible shadow thing had destroyed his home, his people, his god.

"This is the future that comes," said the rattling voice of the old man. "It is you who will prevent it. You who will stop the destruction of your people."

Chapter 1

Moriv's courage struggled with the task ahead of him, but he fought with himself to accept it. He let go of his fear, and felt it drop away. The ancestors had entrusted this duty to him, and he would be worthy of their faith. He took a deep breath and asked, "How can I serve my purpose?"

While he could not see the source of the raspy voice, Moriv felt the old man smile. "There is another blade. One much shorter and simpler. It was forged by the same hand, but it came before the crafting of the sword. This dagger is what you must seek, for it alone has the power to bring down the enemy and prevent the future that you saw."

"Where can I find this dagger?" Moriv asked in earnest.

"In the Tomb of the Betrayer. But to gain access, you will have to fight with both blades and cunning. Even then, the blade is hidden beyond our sight. Tell Konrix what you need, and he will see to it that you are given all that we can provide. Walk in the darkness, child. May the whispers in the night never lead you astray." With that, the voices were gone.

Moriv opened his eyes. His body felt weak, as if he had been working in the field all day with no water. He could only take two breaths before he collapsed under the weight of his exhaustion. Deftly, Konrix leapt forward to catch Moriv before he could fall to the ground. Like a lover, Konrix caressed aside the veil of dark hair that had fallen into Moriv's eyes. "Did they speak to you, Scion?"

Moriv swallowed and smacked his dry mouth, searching for enough fluid to allow the words to escape, finding only just enough for one word, "Water…"

Shadow of the Pyramid

Chapter 2

The people who lived in the shadow of the Great Pyramid talked in hushed whispers about the world beyond. Few had been to the edge of the shadow and seen the brilliant sands that lay beyond the borders of Shatter. One thing all the stories had in common: the painful brightness of the sun.

Moriv stood there on the border of the shadow staring at the blinding world beyond. Surrounding him were the twenty slaves that had been sent as his property for this mission, a mission that was to take him far north of his homeland. None of the people standing there had ever seen the golden sands north of the Pyramid. They stood in awe of the untouched waves of glowing dust before them. It seemed… unnatural.

Ten of the twenty souls in Moriv's possession were the finest warriors of Shatter. The other ten were a mix of porters, workers, and handmaidens. While those first ten were to see to the Scion's protection, it was up to the others to take care of all his other needs. None of the slaves begrudged their duties; quite the opposite. It was the greatest honor to serve the Scion of the Great Obsidian Pyramid. All of them were happy to do even the most menial task, or even give their lives for Moriv. From time to time since he had

Shadow of the Pyramid

been given the slaves, Moriv found himself thinking about how, just weeks ago, he had been a lowly slave himself, and now how he had slaves of his own.

The adjustment to being a master of slaves was harder than Moriv thought it would be. When Konrix told him that he would have company on his journey to the north, Moriv imagined himself as a dispassionate tyrant who would care nothing for the people who were his property. One look from the dark eyes of his handmaidens melted his heart, however. He could not stand to see them grovel at his feet or do some of the disgusting work that Moriv's old master would ask of him. Instead, Moriv wanted to treat his slaves more like friends or companions. While the house slaves liked the feeling that came with this level of recognition, the warriors mostly missed the discipline and the opportunity to bring their fist down on a lesser slave for a minor offense. Konrix counseled Moriv that time and challenges may test the way he treated his slaves. Moriv resented that piece of advice.

Twenty-one souls dressed in silks, leading pack animals laden down with tents and all manner of comforts, and all of them staring with frightened curiosity out into the golden waves before them. Moriv knew that the sun would not hurt him or his brown-skinned companions, yet there was some mischief he felt it was time to make.

He brushed his thin mustache away from his lips before he spoke. "You." He picked out one of the warriors. "Step out of the shadow first and make my introduction to the rest of the world."

"Me?" The warrior asked with eyes wide as saucers.

Moriv just nodded.

The warrior steeled himself against the rays of the sun, which he feared might tear him apart like a swarm of flesh eating insects. He turned toward the land outside of the shadow and closed

Chapter 2

his eyes. One step, then another, and he could feel the heat of the sun upon his flesh. He was braced for the terrible burning pain, but none came. A giant smile came to his face and he pounded his chest. Hollering with exuberant joy, he proclaimed loudly to the empty desert before him, "Beware children of the light! A new Scion of the Great Obsidian Pyramid has come to bring terror into your light filled world. Quake in fear, enemies of our beloved shadow, for Moriv has come to do…" The warrior paused and looked over at Moriv. "What are we out here to do, Master?"

Moriv laughed and applauded the warrior slave with a half mocking clap. Without answering the warrior's question, Moriv slowly stepped through the sand and across the line of shadow into the light of the sun. "I have come to steal the blade of the Betrayer and slay its master," he shouted into the open air beyond. "Now, let us head onward. It is a long way to The Deepening."

The warrior felt somehow as if he had been given special permission to ask more questions and so he blurted out, "What are we to do in The Deepening, Master?"

Moriv felt as if he should have hit the slave for asking him too many questions, as he had always seen other masters do. He decided to let this question go, however, and even to answer it. "There is a tournament there. People from all over the world come to The Deepening to fight for the right to breach the tomb of the Betrayer. We are going there, slave, so that I might enter the tomb and discover how to track down our enemy. Inside its locked walls is the place where the blade was forged. It is there that I shall claim that which is already mine."

The warrior nodded with an approving smile.

"Do not mistake my kindness for weakness, slave. The next time you ask me questions without permission, I will remove your ability to ever ask questions again."

Shadow of the Pyramid

The warrior nodded again and quickly slipped back into his duties of protecting the Moriv and his property.

Moriv and his companions traveled deep into the sands. None of them had been this far from their home before, and all of them would take quick looks over their shoulder to see the black Pyramid slipping farther and farther away. By the end of the first day, the obsidian peak of their god was obscured by distance and dunes of sand.

When night fell, they unfurled the lavish tents and carpets that had been given to Moriv. Together, they reveled in the darkness of the night. A fire was lit in a brazier filled with oil to keep warm the blood of the warriors.

Moriv needed no fire. His blood was so hot with lust and power that he shared that burning with his handmaidens. There, in the darkness of his lush tent, he learned every beautiful thing about the three slaves sent to pleasure him. When he saw the memories of punishments long past etched into their flesh, Moriv decided to distance himself from them. He was, after all, the Scion of the Great Pyramid. Who were these women if not playthings? If he grew to care for them, his mission might be in peril. With a heart made of obsidian, he enjoyed the charms of these women.

When the burning sun rose the next morning, its baleful glare found them already on the move, their fine things packed and carried. Again they were but twenty-one shadows traversing the golden dunes.

Moriv found it quite unnerving that there was no other sign of life that he could see. No traces of footsteps. No buildings or trees. Not even any animals crossed their path. This place is how he imagined that the world might come to an end. The sky filled with fire, the land turned to dust, and a capricious wind that brought relief from the heat, but had invisible claws made of sand. This is

Chapter 2

the world that the Pyramid protected them from. This is what would happen should the obsidian crumble and the light let loose upon all things.

"Master, how do we know we are going the right way?" one of the handmaidens asked from lips dry and dusty.

Moriv wanted to gently wipe away the dust, but he steeled himself against such unexpected kindness. "The ancients guide us, young one, for I am their son, and they have shown me the way."

His words filled all those who travelled with him with a pride, for even here, their god travelled with them. What most of them didn't know was that they were right.

Around Moriv's neck was a tiny shard of the Pyramid. It was in the shape of a teardrop and embraced by silver. The silver chain that it hung upon was fine and long, and allowed the pendant to hang low over Moriv's chest. He would often find himself touching it without thinking about it, and while he wore it, he heard the distant whisperings of the ancients, almost silently guiding him on his journey.

This necklace was called the Cursed Eye of Damnation, and it was a sacred thing passed down to each of the Scions. Even when those Scions who died far from home, the pendant had always found its way back. Moriv did not truly know how the magic worked, but he knew that this thing was now his - and he intended to keep it a secret, especially from his slaves.

More days passed in this way: travel during the day then rest and revelry at night. There was still no sign of any people, still no markings in the sand to denote their passage. As the days rolled on, Moriv grew to find comfort in this loneliness. His slaves, on the other hand, did not. All but the ten warriors began to fear that they

Shadow of the Pyramid

had become lost in the desert. This same challenge did seem to steel the tough and brutal warriors, yet as their resolve was tightened. As a consequence, however, their lust for conflict grew as well.

"Master! Oh, Master! Most terrifying child of the Pyramid. We are lost in this place. We must find more supplies, or we will surely perish," one of the porters exclaimed on the seventh day of travel.

Moriv smiled. He stopped the caravan and looked at this slave while caressing the whispering eye of the Pyramid. "Are you saying you know better than I? For the ancestors are my mother and my father. The Pyramid gave birth to the man you see here." Moriv's anger was rising, and with that, the intensity of his voice. He almost seemed to feed on the fear coming from the slave's face. "I will decide what way we go, and how long we can survive."

All twenty of the caravan drank in the words of their master. Some found this gulp distasteful, and their faces betrayed them.

"Let your fear poison you." Moriv's voice was chilling and quiet, yet all could hear the power in it. "If you have no faith in our mission, and in me, let the Pyramid take back the soul which it granted you. You do not deserve it."

Silence fell over the group, and then Moriv signaled for them to move on.

Night came once again, and the revelry was not so joyous. The warriors were grim, but eager. The maidens were suddenly shy, and the other slaves huddled together in fear.

"Master, some of the slaves are dead," a warrior woke Moriv from his sleep.

The sun burned angrily down at Moriv as he emerged from his tent, but he didn't care about the sun. He was a child of shadows, and the light would not stop him.

Chapter 2

Moriv followed the warrior to the tent for the porter slaves. Two of them lay dead on their mats. Their bodies were slightly shriveled, and all their passages were overflowing with sand. The other slaves were huddled together on the other side of the tent, fearful of both Moriv and their fallen brothers. Joy caused a smile to emerge on Moriv's face, for one of the dead slaves was the one who spoke against him the day before.

"Leave their bodies in the dust, and cast away their burdens too. We do not need them anymore," Moriv commanded the slaves.

One trembling slave crawled forward and pressed his forehead to the sandy mat upon the ground at Moriv's feet. "Master. They were the ones who carried your tent. Surely you will not have us cast that away."

He could not be angry. His curse had cut both ways, as the magic of his people did. These slaves had lost their lives, and he had lost his tent. It is how things should be. "Leave the tent. I do not need it. The sky is beautiful here at night. Why should I hide from it?"

Before they were on their way, they piled up the tent, the lavish mats, and the rest of the slaves' burden and set them ablaze. Thrown like garbage to the side were the bodies of the two slaves, naked and shriveled; they were left for whatever animals lived in this dusty place.

One more day passed, and that night Moriv found himself under the stars. A simple blanket on the ground kept him from lying in the sand. As the night got cold, he found himself kept warm by the shapely bodies of his maidens. The whispering from the stone still echoed in his mind as he drifted off to sleep. His last thought before the darkness took him, "All is how it should be."

Shadow of the Pyramid

The next morning, two more slaves were dead. Their sand-filled and shrivelled bodies were the same as the last two. Again, they burned the things that those slaves carried and travelled onward, leaving the desiccated bodies out for the carrion feeders.

That day the whispering in Moriv's mind grew stronger. His temper was shortened by the bright fire in the sky, for he longed again for the darkness and the stars above. In this fugue of anger at the light, he ignored the whispers telling him which way to go. Many hours of travel passed. In his stubbornness, Moriv started actively leading the caravan the direction that put the sun on their backs. As time stretched on, the whispers grew near screaming in Moriv's head.

With everything that had happened in the last few days, the slaves were hesitant to say anything when Moriv began talking to himself. Even still, they gave their master space when he started separating himself from the group. When madness seemed to grip him, one of the warriors, Junaria, became concerned.

Junaria was an exception among most of the slaves of Shatter. She had a name. The story of how she got her name was a simple one. There was a time, many years ago, when Junaria was a nameless slave in service to the priests of the Mari'Andi. First, it was simple cleaning, but as she matured, the nature of her service changed with the shape of her body. The Scion before Moriv, the very same that had died to give Moriv his power, once called the slave that was Junaria his lover. Before he went on his mission beyond the shadow of the Pyramid, there was an attack that almost took the life of this previous Scion. It seemed that his previous master did not accept that his prized treasure had been taken from him. In a drunken rage, he tried to kill the old Scion, Akreiq, while at a party celebrating the task the Scion was to be set upon.

Chapter 2

The slave who Akreiq called his lover saw the attack coming, and grabbed the glass goblet from the lips of the Scion, broke the glass on the wall near where she sat upon his lap, and drove the large shard that remained in her grasp into the throat of the attacker.

She stood over his gurgling body as he died and spit in the dying man's face. Akreiq began clapping, and it was the only sound in the entire hall at first, for all had hushed the moment she had grabbed for the goblet. Everyone saw the fire in her eyes. Junaria, the Scion called her. He said that it meant moon-fire.

After the Scion left, Konrix put her with the warriors of the temple. And when Moriv became the Scion, she wanted nothing more than to serve him directly. Konrix granted her wish, and she was made the shield of the Scion.

The madness that gripped Moriv troubled Junaria. She feared that he was being tested by the ancestors, and that she too was being tested. At first, the training of a slave came to her. She held her tongue, and subtly looked at the other slaves. They all, even the warriors, had fear in their eyes. After the death of the four slaves at the hands of Moriv's curse, Junaria felt herself steel against her fear. To let the doubt in would be to succumb to the curse. She would not die with her lungs full of sand. This was the warrior in her. The slave and warrior could not find a solution, so she called upon her skills as a lover. She approached Moriv, to the shock of the other slaves, shedding her shield and spear along the way. When she was close enough, she whispered with a lover's whisper, "What haunts you, oh mighty Scion? Let me help you fight the demons that plague you."

Shadow of the Pyramid

Her voice cut through the nightmarish screaming in Moriv's head. For a moment, his thoughts were clear. He turned suddenly towards her, and no longer did he see a faceless slave. Instead he saw the strength of his people personified. She was the dark heart of the Pyramid. She was the ferocious thing which lived in the sideways part of the consciousness of men.

"The stone," he whispered. "The stone wants to rule me. It wants to tell me what I should do. I must resist!"

Closer still she came, and placed her gentle fingers upon his hand that was clenched round the pendant so tightly blood trickled down his arm. "You are the master here, even of the stone. There is no darkness that you do not command. Tell me, what sacrifice do they demand for your divine mission to continue?"

To Moriv's eyes she was a towering shadow with glowing eyes. She was the Night Walker, the legendary ally and protector of the ancestors. "Blood must color the sand. Kill them." Moriv pointed at his three handmaidens. For what did he need them anymore? He had found the fire to keep his very soul warm, and it was her.

Junaria nodded and calmly walked over to the three maidens. The did not seem afraid of her, so she knew that they had not heard what was coming. Slowly, Junaria drew her short blade, the one given to her by Konrix when she joined the warriors of the temple, and with three quick strokes in the air, she cut deeply the throats of all three maidens. Their eyes grew wide as they fell to sand, and red streams flowed down the dune.

The ancients were satisfied in this sacrifice, and the many voices silenced in Moriv's mind. One voice spoke, "Walk against the flow of life, and you will find the depths."

Chapter 2

The web of blood that penetrated the sand quietly grew larger as they all stood staring. Moriv watched the sand soak in the dark red life of his slain handmaidens and had no regrets. The people of Shatter live to serve, and their service was now complete.

Thinking on what the whispers had told him, Moriv ran his eyes up the length of the streams of blood to the opened necks that were their source. He did not stop, he looked up the dune that they were all standing on, and quietly pushed past the silent slaves that waited for his command. They followed him up the dune, and when he reached the peak, the vastness of the desert was stretched out before him. On the horizon, he saw dark clouds. Lightning flickered inside them as they loomed ominously over a dark spot of ground.

Moriv squinted to see what lay in the shadow of the storm, but the distance and the light were against him, so he started walking. Without a single word, the fourteen souls started their trek towards that mysterious stormcloud.

Grey clouds rolled across the sky, and as they collided, sparks crashed to the earth. Peering into the coming storm, Moriv saw shapes on the horizon. With each step, these shapes became clearer, but he could only be sure that they were not more dunes.

A brilliant flash of light came from the sky, and just as the immense boom that followed hit Moriv's ears, he realized what the shapes were. Trees. The horizon was littered with trees and lush grasses. They had finally made it to the Deepening.

Moriv's blood started pumping with wild excitement, and he picked up speed, chasing the storm as it peeled away from the horizon.

Shadow of the Pyramid

The slaves saw the trees too, many of them whispering prayers of thanks to the Pyramid for leading them out of the desert. As their toes reached the fertile soil, Moriv lifted the whispering pendant to his lips and gave it a kiss of gratitude.

Sand became more solid earth as they walked closer to the jungle on the horizon. The trees seemed impossibly tall to the slaves who had never seen their kind before. The bark of the trees looked like a lattice of leaves that had grown together, forming an elaborate armor. Branches reached out from the top of the tree, leaving most of the trunk barren. In the shade of these towering trees were all manner of other bushes, ferns, and shrubs. As the storm clouds receded, the brilliant green of this lush flora dazzled Moriv's caravan.

"This bright world does hold some amazing wonders," Moriv muttered.

"Be careful, Master," Junaria warned. "Do not let this accursed place seduce you away from the shadow."

Moriv felt a little insulted that she would think this place could steal away his heart with wondrous plants. Instead of punishing her, he chuckled. "Things born in this light could never seduce me while I have you to protect me," he whispered to her.

Junaria could not help but let a tiny smile come to her lips.

Before they realized it, they were deep in the lush rocky jungle. Under their feet, the rocks were more solid than the sand dunes, but they were no less treacherous. Whispers from Moriv's stone continued to drive them on through dense plants. Two of the warriors hacked their way through the brush with their swords, blazing a trail for the rest of the group.

Colorful birds and curious monkeys watched with wary eyes from the trees above as Moriv's company pushed their way through the jungle. None of these people of Shatter had ever seen a

Chapter 2

jungle before. Eyes filled with wonder were completely distracted by the terrifying beauty. Stories of the wild creatures that lay in wait outside the protection of the Pyramid haunted their thoughts. Every branch that rustled stirred the paranoia that bubbled to the surface of their minds.

Slowly they creeped in the direction that the stone whispered to Moriv. The fear washed over the group, and the Scion pushed them onwards. Time was running out. He needed to find the camp where he could challenge for the right to get into the tomb of the Betrayer.

"Keep moving!" Moriv shouted. "Faster!"

The slaves complied. Hacking and rushing through the foliage, the fervor of the Pyramid's Scion drove them on. Cutting and slashing, branches and leaves became the carpet on which Moriv walked, his slaves slicing their way to his victory. Moriv smiled a wicked smile and felt invincible. One more chop, and suddenly the slave out in front seemed to disappear, then the second slave vanished.

The whole train of them stopped, because the third slave held up his hand signaling them to halt. The slave in the back of the group could not see, and he stumbled into the group, pushing the warrior who called for the group to stop off the edge of the cliff, and his dying screams echoed off the canyon as he fell beyond their sight.

This hidden edge of the land above had claimed three lives from Moriv, but still his heart burned with a furious need for victory. He pushed his way passed his slaves and the wild foliage. Standing there at the edge, he knew then why they called this chasm The Deepening. This massive gash in the earth stretched to his

Shadow of the Pyramid

left and right farther than he could see, and was wide enough to fit many Pyramids. The sheer immensity of this hole in the earth made Moriv smile.

All the unnamed slaves stared at Moriv with wary fear in their faces. The Scion, still burning with the will of the ancients, grabbed a thick vine and after testing its strength, he began his descent.

For what seemed like hours, the small group from Shatter climbed down the damp rocky surface. Jutting stones and sinuous vines bore them ever downward. Moriv took small note of the broken fragments of fallen warriors as he climbed past them, but the other slaves would pause briefly to pray for their fallen brothers, and to wish they did not have to leave their beasts of burden behind at the top of the cliff. When they reached the bottom, they found the largest pieces of the torn corpses of those warrior slaves that had plummeted to their death. Junaria roared at some dog sized lizards that were rapidly devouring the flesh of her sword brothers. With a hiss, the lizards fled from the ferocious servant of the Scion.

Junaria knelt where she could see all three of the remains and whispered, "Brothers, may you find your reward in the cold arms of our ancestors, and may I not be quick to follow you." Dipping her fingers in their blood, she drew a triangle on her shield.

Moriv watched this ceremony with a curious wonder. Slaves in Shatter did sometimes hold vigil for the dead, but those with names never mourned for the nameless. Even with this break in tradition, Moriv silently approved of the ceremony that was performed, and when the other slaves looked to him with nervous stares, he just nodded at them to let them know it was ok. When Junaria was finished with her remembrance of the fallen, Moriv let the whispers from the stone drive him deeper into the jungle.

Chapter 2

Danger dripped from every shadow. It rustled from every branch. This jungle wanted Moriv and his slaves to nourish its roots. Moriv ignored the fear the gripped the hearts of his slaves. He used Junaria's fearlessness and the whispering of the stone to keep him going. The deeper they got within the basin of the valley, the more Moriv embraced the ferocious animal that lay quiet in his heart.

Junaria knew that something, or rather some things, were stalking the group. As the light from the sun waned from the sky, the humid struggle against the light was replaced with avoiding the predators that were waking up to find food. The path they were cutting in to the Jungle was leaving a visible trail, one that could easily be followed. Junaria did not encourage those in front to stop hacking at the jungle; she wanted to see what this place had to offer, apart from twisting vines and hidden cliffs. She wanted to shed the blood of this place.

In the twilight of the valley, they could hear the violent deaths of things in their wake. The predators were feeding on the distracted prey who were avoiding these strangers from the Pyramid. The screeching death rattles of these animals caused ripples in the branches of the trees. These waves hit the morale of the slaves, filling their hearts with doubt yet again. The curse that Moriv had placed upon his own people had not yet done its worst.

Night fell, and Moriv insisted that the group press on. Slowly they crept through the jungle with no light, save the stars above.

The first slave to disappear must have stepped on a hive of bugs and been distracted by the biting insects, because he never heard the beasts come for him. The second to die was a warrior that saw something to the side and decided to check on it without saying

Shadow of the Pyramid

a word. One by one, Moriv's doubting, fearful slaves were picked off behind him, as Junaria and he eagerly pushed forward through the bush.

Junaria finally noticed that their numbers had been cut down to only four when she stopped to truly assess why the group was making less noise. "What happened to the others?" she whispered to the slaves behind her. They only shrugged and made some vague motion at the jungle around them.

She then knew that the fight she hoped for was coming. She would shed blood this night, and it would be glorious. Taking her place at the back of the group, in her heart she challenged the jungle to do its worst.

Long enough the beasts had waited. To them, Moriv shone like a beacon of life, one that they could not resist. Like cunning moths who seek to steal a flame, they stalked him, ignoring the other humans. As the first one of these reptilian beasts crashed through the brush and lunged at Moriv, it received a swipe across the snout from Junaria's blade.

"Master! You are under attack!" she shouted boldly.

Moriv smiled and quickly drew his blade, He, too, had been waiting for a fight. He had yet to use the blade given to him by Konrix. Now it was time for Shadow Stealer to take lives, as it was meant to.

The blade was not new, and Moriv was not the only Scion to have wielded it. The last time it had been used was in a war against the Princes of Broken. So long had the rivalry gone on between the city of Broken and the chosen of Shatter, that only their masters remembered the cause.

Chapter 2

The first time it was wielded by a Scion of the temple, however, it was upon a field of battle, where the Pyramid itself had travelled. It had floated up off the great plaza and moved north across the desert, an army of slaves were all safe from the light inside the belly of this massive shadow. When the two armies met, their clash tore apart the very earth, causing it to rip and collapse beneath their might. The Pyramid itself shots glimmering rays of light that caused a deep chasm to open in the earth, swallowing half of the army that stood against it.

The Princes of Broken were not without their own powers, however, and they launched great stones into the air with machines of war. Hundreds of them pelted the Pyramid, and eventually their endless assault caused cracks within the obsidian. The first of these cracks send a shockwave of sound across the battlefield, causing all combatants to cease their clash, even just for that moment, to stare in awe at what was happening.

Great tendrils of light and darkness leaked forth from the cracks in the Pyramid, licking the air and entwining across the surface of the Pyramid itself. The Scion, who was at this battle, was standing so near the Pyramid when it cracked that the sound alone knocked him to the ground. When he saw what had happened, his heart was filled with such rage that he picked up a long shard of the Pyramid, one that was shaped like a blade, and started running towards the enemy's battle line.

As he ran, he was able to make out where the seven Princes of Broken were standing, back behind their army. He sliced his way through the combat towards them. So great was their arrogance that they just stood there, waiting for him to arrive. As he approached, the Princes just smiled. Their near black skin was covered in

Shadow of the Pyramid

brightly colored silks, the best that their limitless coffers could buy. All of them were identical, save for tiny differences in their clothes and jewelry.

This ancient Scion suddenly was confused, for they all looked like the same man. All of them smiled at him with the same unflinching malice. Unsure what to do, the Scion just lashed out at the nearest of the Princes to him, slicing the prince across the cheek. Suddenly, all seven of the Princes were animated by their anger and attacked the Scion with knives, swords, and spears.

The battle only lasted a few moments, and the blade never touched another of the Princes that night. The Scion had made his mark and was left to rot upon the field after the chasm grew to separate the two armies enough that they could no longer continue their fight.

Years later, the blade was reclaimed by a different Scion who had been tasked to return it to the Pyramid, and it was shaped and changed from the crude shard into a masterpiece of dark glass. The silver handle was etched so finely that the detail of the design faded from view when anyone was not looking close upon it, and was done specifically to prevent the silver from outshining the obsidian blade.

As Moriv drew the sword with murderous intent, the story of its making was whispered to him by the stone that was leading him on his journey. He reeled as his mind took on the overwhelming memories of the previous Scion, and he struggled to get back to his feet once it was over.

When Moriv returned to his senses, he saw that Junaria and the two other warriors had killed one of the massive reptiles. Still two more of the hulking things, with terrible maws filled with dagger length teeth, still sought human flesh to fill their bellies.

Chapter 2

One of the beasts lunged at Junaria as she quickly brought up her shield to bash the creature's snout. Shooting a glance over at Moriv, she shouted, "Master Scion! Are you ok?"

Before he could respond, Moriv heard the crackling passage of something coming through the jungle behind him. Looking over his shoulder, he saw another of the reptilian monsters. This one had stalked around the Scion's protectors to try and collect an easy feast. Moriv tightened his grip on Shadow Stealer as he turned to face the creature. The two opponents let loose roars at the same time and charged to meet one another.

The company from Shatter was fighting for their very lives, but not against the treacherous tyrants of Broken, Flay, or of the other nations of the world. Instead they were locked in a battle with the denizens of this deep dank jungle. The humidity was unlike anything they were used to, and it was stealing their very strength. As they danced their way through the fight, streams of sweat poured down their backs and off their brows. The very air was pressing on their will to continue fighting.

A fog of exhaustion began to fill their minds, and one of the warriors suddenly found that his body would no longer listen. One tiny delay in dodging a lunging bite, and the warrior's left shoulder found its way into the maw of one of the beasts. He screamed in agony as his ribcage was shattered under the force of the creature's jaws, and a shower of blood sprayed everyone. Knowing he was dead, the warrior jabbed his sword into the eye of his killer, blinding the beast and causing it to shake him violently.

Junaria dodged a dismembered arm that went flying by her, hitting the lizard facing her. She and the other remaining warrior took that brief moment to score a hit against the side of the creature's neck, causing it to give a screeching wail. It recovered quickly from the wound and resumed its attack.

Shadow of the Pyramid

The blinded reptile began feasting on the unmoving corpse of the slain warrior, throwing gore in every direction as it tore through the flesh and shattered bones. The feasting distracted the hungry beast that had engaged Moriv, and it disengaged to try and steal some meat from the fallen warrior. Shadow Stealer had scored a few light hits against this beast, and Moriv could only think that the reptile had decided against pressing the attack on him further. Moriv instead turned his attention to the beast that his companions were fighting.

The three of them cornered the reptile, and with Junaria blocking its attacks, Moriv got in a few quick slashes to its side and underbelly, wounding it severely.

As the Scion and Junaria moved in to finish off the dying monster, the other warrior turned and found the remaining two beasts hissing at each other over the ravaged corpse between them. They took snapping bites at each other in an attempt to chase the other away from the torn flesh.

Believing he had an opportunity to score a fatal blow on one of the creatures, the warrior leapt forward. His timing could have been better, for as he came into range, the two lizards both turned on him and attacked. One dug its dagger-long teeth into his upper sword arm, the other bit into the top part of his shield, and together they pulled him in different directions with such force that the straps on his shield broke, and in doing so his shield arm's wrist nearly exploded, sending bones from his forearm through the surface of his skin. There was a wet ripping sound as the other beast tore his sword arm off his body. Shocked and in pain, the warrior screamed and fell to his knees. As the one beast was distracted by the fresh meat of his arm, the other recoiled for another attack, and brought its powerful jaws down over the head of the kneeling warrior. There was another muffled cracking and a spray of blood

Chapter 2

as the beast's maw crushed the warrior's torso. With a violent shake, the reptile tore away the corpse's head and chest, leaving behind the shield arm, half the torso, and legs to fall twitching to the ground.

Shadow Stealer finally tasted the heartsblood of the fallen beast. Moriv and Junaria turned to find their companions torn to shreds and the two remaining beasts rapidly devouring their flesh and bones.

There was a moment where Moriv considered sneaking off into the jungle, but that thought never crossed Junaria's mind. She let loose a roar and charged the nearest beast, slamming into it with her shield and nearly knocking it off balance. Moriv followed her lead, and found himself relishing in the rush that the combat gave him. He plunged Shadow Stealer deep into the side of the unbalanced creature's neck, and the puncture caused a fountain of blood to pour freely from the wound.

Without wasting a moment, Junaria turned to the second creature and found it already charging at her. She raised her shield in time to block the charging attack, but as the creature crashed into her, it also lifted its head, knocking her backwards onto the ground.

That moment was the first time Junaria had actually felt fear. On her back, with her arms spread out, she lifted her head to see the menacing thing staring at her prone body. She quickly realized that she was laying amidst the gore of her fallen companions, causing a slippery problem should she try and stand up too fast.

As the wounded beast lunged at Moriv again, he slashed at the snout of the thing, opening a huge tear in the beast's flesh with Shadow Stealer. As the creature screeched and recoiled from Moriv, the Scion stepped forward. He drove the black tip of Shadow Stealer into the neck of the beast over and over, until the thing fell over writhing and bleeding.

Shadow of the Pyramid

Junaria rolled away from the first charge of the beast who had knocked her over, but when she tried to stand up, again she got caught by a charge which knocked her back off her feet. The beast was persistent and continued to pursue her, ignoring Moriv's killing of the other massive reptile. It charged her again, and she was able to bring her shield up just in time to block the attack, wedging the shield sideways into the creature's wide open mouth. Before it could even pull away from her, she used her sword to cut away the leather strap on the shield and released it just in time to avoid the powerful beast's attempt to shake the shield loose from its jaws.

Moriv turned away from the dying lizard to find the other beast trying to pry the wedged shield from its jaws. On the other side of it, Junaria stood. They gave each other a look and a nod to signal that they were unharmed, and then they both closed on the beast. Just before they got within striking distance, the beast crushed the shield in its jaws, sending huge splinters of wood in every direction. Moriv sent Shadow Stealer point first into the creature's side, and the beast wheeled around and smashed into Moriv with the side of its head, knocking the Scion into the air.

The creature hissed at Moriv before preparing to pounce, a pounce that was cut short by another strike from behind as Junaria pierced its other flank. The beast roared a powerful roar that made the leaves on the trees rustle.

Junaria, swinging wild, powerful swings at the creature, kept it both distracted and at bay long enough for Moriv to get back to his feet. Quietly, he walked up to the creature and again struck from behind, and as it turned, Junaria did the same. Again the creature howled and turned, and again Moriv struck it from behind. Moriv and Junaria took turns stabbing the distracted beast that could not make up its mind which one of them to attack. Its

Chapter 2

indecision would ultimately be its undoing, and in the end Moriv and Junaria stood there looking at each other across the pile of perforated flesh at their feet.

They were both covered in blood and exhausted. Moriv's mind cried out for water, but his body was slow to react. Before he could move, light from torches filled the small grove in the jungle, and people all from different styles of dress stood before them. They were all armed and looked ready for a fight.

The men looked around at the carnage before them and some of them were suddenly very afraid. A man with skin as dark as pitch spoke.

"We heard noises in the jungle, and thought that someone might be out here getting eaten. It seems that we were not wrong," he said, gesturing to the two dismembered corpses of men.

Moriv looked at them all blankly. He was so tired, he barely cared who they were.

"You speak to the Scion of the Great Obsidian Pyramid," Junaria said as she stepped between the men and Moriv.

The black-skinned man smiled, "Has the Scion come to fight in the games, then? We men of the Free City of Broken would happily face him in combat."

"Can he not speak for himself?" a mocking voice called from the crowd.

Junaria casually picked up the intact shield that lay at her feet, she slipped out the dismembered arm that was still gripping the handle and waited for the situation to decide what it wanted to be.

"He has come to fight," Moriv said powerfully. "Have you come to show us to the arena?"

Shadow of the Pyramid

One of the other men, wearing an off-white tabard with a single wide green stripe riding over his armor, stepped forward, "This we can do for you, m'lord Scion." The man bowed. His skin was pale, and he had the look of death about him. Moriv had heard of the revenants of Flay. Could this be one? The man spoke again, "Follow us and we will take you the rest of the way. We are nearly there."

Moriv nodded, and after Junaria had a few moments of prayer over her fallen warrior brothers, the last two souls that had set out from Shatter went on their way.

Chapter 3

The camp was larger and more lavish than Moriv had expected, so much so that he could scarcely call it a camp. It was much more like a little town. The sections of the town were separated by fences and were filled with a mixture of tents and permanent structures. It was like a small civilized eye in the middle of the storm that was the jungle.

When they arrived it was night, and fires were lit up and down the little town, lighting the various sections. Everything about this place seemed planned and structured. The placement of the buildings, the streets made in straight lines, even the very ground the town was built upon were as flat as the great plaza in Shatter. Moriv thought about the countless hours it would have taken to tame the jungle to create this oasis.

Banners were hung at the entrance to every section that surrounded the Theatre of Blood, a shallow coliseum in the middle of the town. The arena floor of smoothly carved marble almost looked like a pool of water in the flickering light of torches from the street. They passed the dark purple banner of Onisvaal, the nation that called the Free City of Broken its capital. It was emblazoned with the seven crowns of the Princes of Onisvaal. At this camp that the shadow-skinned men left the group that had escorted Moriv to the little town.

Shadow of the Pyramid

"See you in the morning, Scion," the man said in a hollow, but pleasant tone. "Perhaps we will see your blood on the floor of the theatre."

The other men from Onisvaal chuckled at Moriv, but he paid them no attention. In truth, he was glad to be rid of them.

"I understand that your people have a disagreement with the people of Broken," the revenant that was leading them said.

Moriv just shrugged. He was not about to open his heart to this undead man he did not know. As far as he was concerned, Junaria was the only person here he could trust.

The revenant nodded. "I understand. Just keep this in mind: in this place, there is only one area that has rules, and that is the arena. There are no kings, barons, princes, or prophets here."

The group of them came to a fenced-in section that was completely empty and slightly overgrown. A post outside the low stone fence had a black Pyramid atop it. It was here that the revenant said his farewell, and left Moriv and Junaria standing alone.

The Scion felt foolish for leaving the lavish tents in the desert. Further, he cursed his mind for forgetting the rest of their supplies in the jungle with the dead warriors.

Junaria set right to work cleaning out a tiny section of the overgrown bushes and grass to create a nest where they could rest, and Moriv joined her in the effort. Before the sun had come up, they had something small, and deep enough in the brush that it was hidden. Once they had this nest, they celebrated their survival by enjoying each other's bodies under the night sky.

When morning came, the sun's rays callously forced them awake. The rest of the town had already come to life, and it felt much more like a little city.

Chapter 3

Moriv and Junaria went out into the crowd to take in their surroundings and try and find some supplies. It was likely that the group from Onisvaal had supplies for sale, as their entire empire was built on trade, coin, and greed, but Moriv and Junaria wanted nothing to do with them. Those selfish merchants from Broken likely to sell them poisoned food. The silent war between Shatter and Broken knew no boundaries.

The people of this place were as varied as the banners that hung from the numerous posts around the little town. Some prefered to dress lavishly, like the people of Onisvaal. Other groups dressed more practically, like the pale skinned people of Flay. Moriv had never seen people with skin and eyes unlike the light brown skin and black hair of the children of the pyramid. In that moment the world was a wondrous place filled with all the colors of people he could imagine. He was suddenly curious if there were any blue people, but his rumbling stomach distracted him.

Even though he was hungry, Moriv took some time to watch the many challenges that were occurring in the arena. The multiple combats varied in number and skill of the participants. He wasn't sure quite what to make of the rules. No one was fighting to the death, and sometimes they fought with leather-wrapped weapons instead of sharp-edged ones.

A white scrawny man with long hair pulled loosely into a ponytail came and stood next to Moriv while he was watching. He stood silently for a while, then between bouts he turned to Moriv and said, "You're the Scion of the Obsidian Pyramid, yeah? I'm Darvin, from Skullspill."

Moriv knew the name of the city, and that is was ruled by another of the great masters of the world, one known only as The Baron. Skullspill was otherwise unknown to Moriv, and his wariness came across when he said, "My name is Moriv."

Shadow of the Pyramid

"Great to meet you, Moriv," Darvin said, smiling. "You settling in okay? Need anything?"

"Actually, we lost most of our supplies on the journey here," Moriv said casually.

"Oh I see! Well, that does put you in a bit of a bind, eh?" Darvin rubbed his chin. "I believe that I could probably scrounge up a bit of supply for you, if you were interested."

Junaria gave Moriv a stern look, expressing her mistrust of the situation.

"And what would be the cost of these supplies, Darvin?" Hesitation was heavy in the pace of Moriv's words.

Darvin chuckled a bit. "Calm down, Scion. I have no interest in seeing you lose any fights you have coming up. Just the opposite, I assure you. I have no love for those bastards from Onisvaal either." Darvin's tone went dark, "I would love to see them all burn, truth be told."

Moriv smiled. "What of your master, The Baron? Does he not care for the Princes?"

With eyes rolling Darvin replied, "Oh, aye. I am sure that the Red Lord cares about the Princes. But I am not here on behalf of him, you see."

Moriv was confused. In Shatter there was only one cause to care about, the will of the Pyramid. The idea that this man from Skullspill did not care for The Baron actually made Moriv hesitate.

"Ya know," Darvin continued, "The Red Lord and the Mari'Andi have not always gotten along. In fact, one might say that he prefers the company of our black skinned friends over there to the children of the Pyramid. My employer would see that change."

"Employer? Is that like your master?" Moriv found the ways of people outside the shadow of the Pyramid to be confusing.

Chapter 3

"Something like that, yeah. I suppose," Darvin paused. "Listen, if you don't want to do business with me, or my employer, we can all walk away friends. No harm done. But if you want an ally here in this camp - you might want to start somewhere. No one from Shatter has been here to compete in any history I have ever heard. Still, someone made sure that they had a section carved out for them. I have been here for at least the last five of these tournaments. No one ever makes it inside the tomb. People just use it as an excuse for glory, assassination, and making money. Trust me, friend, I stand to make a lot more from you winning than I do from you dying."

"Bets? You are betting on the Scion?" Junaria blurted out, which came as a surprise, even to her, though her demeanor would never show that.

"Yes, actually," Darvin said flatly. "These games have been going on for at least a hundred years. If the Pyramid has sent one of their famed Scions here, I don't feel like there is any way I could turn down that bet."

Moriv finally understood what this man wanted from him. He wasn't interested in anything other than winning the betting game that was on the side. What was the harm in taking some of his supplies, if he stood to gain from Moriv's victory? The Pyramid did not send him here for glory or for money.

"Fine. I will take your supplies, Darvin of Skullspill. And I will make sure you win your bet."

Darvin's face lit up like a full harvest moon. "Right then! I will send some of my folks over to your area to help set things up. You will know that they are my folks if they say that Mariano sent them."

"Who is Mariano?" asked Moriv.

Darvin smiled. "My employer." With that he walked away.

Shadow of the Pyramid

Moriv started paying more attention to the people in the town. It seemed that very few of them were here for the actual challenges, and that most people were here as part of a sort of nomadic village. There were merchants of every variety; food, clothing, weapons, even slaves were all for sale. This makeshift little town was very colorful indeed. More than one disagreement led to the shedding of blood away from the marble arena. Most of them were petty, foolish arguments that would often end in the death of one or more people. Moriv could not help but dwell on the miserable lives that people must live to kill each other over selfish, fleeting greed and glory. His life had more meaning than that.

At one end of the arena, he saw some black-robed people changing out tokens on a large board. Each token was distinct, but they sometimes repeated on the board's odd network of groupings.

"What is this board?" Moriv asked one of the robed figures.

The woman took back her hood and smiled at him, "Good day to you, Scion."

"Word of you has traveled fast, Master," Junaria said quietly.

"This board is where the score will be kept for the great contest," the woman continued.

"How does it work?" Moriv asked.

The woman smiled. "We create pairings for the fights, Scion. Each match is fought in the styling decided by the competitors, though usually it is to five hits. Two points are scored if the hit actually draws blood, and that blood touches the marble floor of the arena."

"Do people ever fight to the death?"

Chapter 3

The woman nodded. "Yes, Scion. Though it is rare. Both combatants must agree. Death caused by accident will disqualify the one who caused the death."

"I see," Moriv said quietly.

The woman continued, trying to lighten the mood. "Just because one loses a match with the bound blades does not mean one is out. All combatants will face each other at least once before fighters will be eliminated."

"How many opponents are there?" Moriv asked.

"That is a fine question, Scion." The woman reached for a scrap of parchment at the base of the board. "It appears that there are nine entries. Apart from yourself, there is Gorand from the Free City of Broken; Lady Klenni Bonewraith, knight of Skullspill; Master Cecil Everbright, Painwarden of Flay; Marks Haas, citizen of the lost town of Marrowdale; Jonathan Windhold of Yellow Liver; Murgallis, Champion of his Majesty, King Raax of the Frozen Waste; Yarenti of the Shadow Hunters; and Kraatic, Servant of The Mistress of the Rise."

"Frozen Waste? The Rise?" Moriv wondered aloud.

The woman smiled. "Yes. We are fortunate to have non-human combatants this year. It will certainly be exciting."

"What else should I know?" Moriv wasn't sure what else to ask.

The woman paused to think. "Um. Oh! After the first round, those who have the highest number of wins are matched against the lowest for a second round, wherein the losers are eliminated. That is what these groupings are for." She gestured at the board. "Then the winners of matched contests get matched against one another until there is only one winner."

"Why have I been seeing group competitions in the arena?" Moriv asked.

Shadow of the Pyramid

The woman laughed. "Well, before the actual competition, people like to warm up the arena with matches for betting purposes, but matches can include more than one combatant if both sides agree. In those cases, the number of hits eliminates an combatant, and the desired number of hits against the primary participant will end the match."

Junaria laughed. "Why would anyone do that? So they can hide behind their larger friends?"

The woman quickly answered, "It has happened before that way, yes. Those bouts are rare and unpredictable."

Moriv had heard enough; he needed food and a good night's sleep before the fights began. Fighting with padded weapons did not make him or Shadow Stealer very happy, but he knew he would have to play by their rules. "Thank you for your help, lady."

"Ingri. Ingri of the Eternal Well." She smiled and went back to working on the scoreboard.

As they walked away, Junaria asked, "Who are the Eternal Well?"

Moriv shrugged. "I have no idea. These children of the sun are all very strange."

They arrived back at their section to find that the bushes had been cleared and the grounds prepared for the large tent that was being erected before them. Moriv was shocked at first, and then remembered the question he should ask.

"Hey, you there," he shouted at a large man working on unfolding the canvas top of the large tent. "Who is it that sent you?"

The man looked over both his shoulders and waited patiently for a passerby to leave hearing range before replying, "Mariano sent me."

Moriv smiled. It was good to have friends, even if they were obviously criminals in some far away land.

48

Chapter 3

Before long the tent was standing, providing plenty of shade. The inside had a floor with lush carpet and silk draperies. Fruit and dried meats were laid out in bowls, along with wine and water. Darvin had seemingly spared no expense, as this was the life the decadent priests of the Mari'Andi were accustomed to. Moriv had had just a taste of this life before he left Shatter, but it already felt a little more like home.

Again, he and Junaria celebrated their lives with loud and joyous coupling under their opulent tent. The morning would start the contest that would lead to Moriv's destiny, but that night was for filling his soul with fire.

"Oi!" The voice shattered Moriv's dreams and forced his body to movement.

His eyes struggled to open. When his heavy lids were lifted, Moriv saw Junaria with a blade to the throat of the large man who helped erect his tent. Beyond him, the burning light of the day was just outside the tent opening. Worry gripped Moriv. "What time is it?" he asked, leaping up to get dressed.

Ignoring his question, Junaria replied, "This man tried to sneak into your tent, Scion."

"I came out 'ere to make sure you wasn't dead! Not ta kill ya." The man slowly pushed the blade away from his throat. "My boss would flay me alive and throw me into the sewers of Skullspill if I murdered ya."

"It is okay, Junaria. He speaks the truth," Moriv calmed her.

The man straightened his spine as Junaria backed away from him. "You's already a bit late, but you didn't miss much."

"What do you mean I am late?" Moriv's tone was suddenly angry.

Shadow of the Pyramid

Junaria lifted the tip of her blade, and the man raised his empty hands in a defensive posture. "Easy! Like I said, you didn't miss nuffin. Just some of the early fights. There were some delays..."

"Delays?" Junaria asked.

The man's eyes darted back and forth between Junaria and Moriv a few times before he spoke, "Yeah. First two fights caused a bit of a ruckus, you might say. First thing, that Champion of Raax comes out and it wasn't what people expected, it was a human!"

"What did people expect?" Moriv asked, as he started putting on pieces of his finely tooled leather armor.

"Well, I dunno really. The people of the Frozen Waste are just a story in Skullspill. They talks about them like they are short little crafty things. Gnomes they call them. But no one 'as ever seen one of 'em."

The main paused, thinking Moriv was distracted with putting on his armor, but when the Scion stopped and looked up at him, he realized he should continue. "Oh! So out comes the champion of Raax, and it is this human fella. From where I was sittin', I could see that there was something off 'bout the way he was movin' though. Then I saw the collar around his neck, like a dog or somefink."

The mention of a collar made Moriv think of home. In Shatter, some slaves would wear collars. Usually it was a sign of station and ceremony, if the collar was finely made. However, there were slaves who would wear collars out of shame or as a punishment. "Are the people of the Frozen Waste known for having slaves?"

Chapter 3

The man shook his head. "I dunno, Master Scion. I will tell ya this though - I don't just think he was a slave. I think his mind was completely controlled by somefink else. His eyes were solid white, and his movements were all strange, like he was a bug or a bird or somefink."

Junaria's eyebrow went up. "Strange."

"Anyways, the fight was a fast one, if you ask me. He fought that fella from Flay, somefink Everbright. Weird name, like all them Flayers. That Champion fella knew what he was doing, alright. And when Everbright kneeled down to salute him on his win, the Champion put a collar on that Flayer's neck!"

"He what?" Moriv was shocked. "That cannot be part of the competition."

The man shook his head. "Nah. As soon as it happen'd though, everyone went mad. All the rest of the Flayers hopped into the arena all yelling and stuff. That Champion slave fella, he just stood there and watched them as they tried to get the necklace off that Everbright guy. That is when swords started to get drawn, but before a fight could get started, them Well people came on and stopped everyfink. They spoke in some strange language to the Champion, and he took back the collar. It was crazy."

Moriv felt unprepared for anything like that. He had come prepared to fight one on one for the chance to enter the tomb, and now he wasn't sure he truly understood the game. "Did the people keeping score do anything else?"

"Oh yeah. They disqualified that Champion of Raax from the fights, and that Everbright guy ain't well enough to keep competin'," the man went quiet for a second, then he continued, "'Course, then after a few more fights, there was the Darakka and the Shadow Hunter. If you ask me, them Shadow Hunters are just a problem. I dunno why they let them compete."

51

Shadow of the Pyramid

"Oh?" Moriv was nearly done with his armor, but he wanted to be aware of everything that had already taken place.

"Yeah. That Shadow Hunter pulled a real blade and just started killin' that Darakka thing. You ever see one of them?"

"A Shadow Hunter?" Moriv hadn't. He wasn't even sure who they were, exactly. He had some vague idea that they were people who fought against The King and The Baron ages ago and were nearly wiped out.

"Nah, a Darakka."

Moriv shook his head. "Can't say I have."

The man grinned. "Tall things they are. Covered in scales, with a head like a crocodile or somefink. Look scary, they do. Like a man mixed with a dragon. Course, dragons aren't real."

The stone whispered to Moriv. He suddenly saw images of massive winged things flying in the sky, raining fire and lightning down on a city like Shatter. The images were frightening and confusing, but they conveyed the message - dragons were very real. Shaking the thoughts from his mind he asked, "What happened then?"

"Oh! That Shadow Hunter started screaming somefink about Sanctuary and somefink about a mistress. No one moved until after the Darakka was layin' there dead. Brutal fight though, don't want to give ya the wrong impression. That Hunter left the pit leavin' a trail of blood behind. As she walked away, the Well people called out her name and before they could say anything else she shouted at 'em, 'I withdraw'. Firey that one. From the look of her though, I wouldn't be surprised if she was dead come morning. Nasty things them Darakka, claws uzkin' cleaved through her armor they did."

Chapter 3

"So that is four out of nine competitors already eliminated?" Moriv asked, mostly to confirm there were no other casualties that he didn't know about.

The man nodded, and said nothing else.

Five competitors remained. Moriv knew he couldn't lose. He was here on a holy mission for his god, his ancestors, and his people. No mindslave of the north, or crazed woman of a fallen people would stop him. Some few months ago, he had just been a common slave, not even a warrior slave. Now, he was about to go into an arena and take on masters of martial crafts, and he wasn't even a little bit afraid.

The three of them walked out of the tent. First, the man stepped out and causally went his own way, then Junaria stepped out and screamed into the tiny town, "Behold, you here at the Theatre of Blood, the Scion of The Great Obsidian Pyramid!"

As Moriv stepped out of the tent, all eyes were on him. It was like this everywhere he went in Shatter after he was made Scion, so he was used to it. Some people in the crowd even bowed. Two sections over, he could hear the mocking laughter of the people from Onisvaal. Their greed and pride blinded them from the truth of Moriv's power. Soon they would know different.

Several hours passed. Before it was time for dinner, Moriv had fought all the preliminary fights against the remaining competitors. He had won his fights against Jonathan Winterhold of Yellow River and Marks Haas of Marrowdale. While his fight against Jonathan seemed urgent and desperate, the fight against Marks made Moriv feel like his opponent was either sizing him up or showing off, maybe even that Marks let him win.

Shadow of the Pyramid

That uncertainty caused him to lose the fight against Klenni Bonewraith, much to the disappointment of Mariano's men. After a pep talk from Darvin that included the comment, "If you don't win, Scion, you aren't any good to me."

Not so subtle threats from Darvin put Moriv a little more off center, and the next match against Gorand was difficult. To Moriv and the people of Shatter, this was the fight that mattered, and yet Gorand was strong, quick, and bursting with pride. Insults flew from Gorand's dark lips, and his wicked smile taunted Moriv. Early on, Gorand pulled ahead in the scoring, and Moriv knew he could not let that happen. Anger began to fuel the Scion's strikes, and their fight went on for a long time.

After multiple clashes, the score was finally tied.

Gorand had never been a slave. He had never known the fierce end of a pacifier's leather cudgel. His life was filled with luxury and decadence. These long duels against Moriv had taken their toll on Gorand's speed and his strength. In the very last clash, it seemed to Junaria that Moriv actually began to toy with Gorand, and it made her quietly chuckle.

With a quick strike to the chest as Gorand lunged, the fight was suddenly over. Moriv had won, and Gorand did not take the loss well.

"I will kill you, and your dog of a woman. Like the obsidian rubble you worship, you are a worthless and fragile bauble. We will see who the real champion is tomorrow," Gorand hissed at Moriv.

Moriv just smiled. "All your gold cannot buy you victory. Go soak in your pride - tomorrow I will take your life."

Gorand's eyes went wide with rage, "I accept. If we fight each other tomorrow, it will be to the death!" As he stormed away, his companions cheered and mocked Moriv.

Chapter 3

Junaria cleared a path to their tent with her worry crushed deep inside her gut. Something was not right. There would be a price for the Scion's pride. She feared it would be her price to bear.

There was no coupling that night. Junaria pushed off the advances of the Scion. Her heart was steeled and focused on the day ahead. As she pushed his hand away from her thigh, she said, "Scion, tonight I must stay alert. That Gorand from Broken will murder you in your sleep, and you have no one else to watch you."

Moriv was disappointed. He wanted to celebrate his victory with the passion that burned inside him, but he knew she was right. Gorand's pride had been too wounded in the theatre, so instead of convincing her to change her mind, he rolled over and went to sleep.

The night was long for Junaria. She could hear the people who were celebrating out in the town around the Theatre of Blood, drunk with their victory, or the release that defeat brought. She could feel the air was filled with bad decisions. Occasionally, there were raised voices and the sounds of a scuffle. Each time she stood and prepared herself to defend the sleeping Scion. Oh, how she longed to be curled up next to him.

Her thoughts turned to how soft life had been in Shatter. There was struggle, yes, but never was she in a situation like this. The games the people of Onisvaal played were nothing like that in the whole of her nation. Dius may have been mostly made of the city of Shatter, but it rarely had these murderous games.

Time passed and the night grew darker and quieter. Perhaps her master was safe after all. Perhaps Gorand's pride would not lead to cowardly murder.

Shadow of the Pyramid

Junaria did not hear the man sneak into the tent, but the tip of his knife she certainly noticed when the pain shot through her side. When she turned, she found herself facing an dark skinned man holding two knives. The look on his face told her that he was surprised his strike to her kidney hadn't put her down.

Fire surged through Junaria's veins. This man had been sent to murder Moriv in his sleep. Her tired mind grew concerned about the Scion, and she looked over at him to make sure he was alright. She could see no wounds and no blood soaking into the mat upon the floor.

While the large woman was distracted, the assassin decided to take a second strike, this time for the heart. His serrated dagger pierced the woman's armor and plunged deep into her flesh, but she gave almost no sound of anguish or pain. The assassin thought his work was done, and release his grip on the dagger to let her die out of range to counterattack or grasp him.

Junaria reeled from the strike to her chest. She could feel the wind leaving her body and despite all her strength, she could not recall it. Gasping for breath, she fell to one knee and watched as the assassin's gaze turned to Moriv. Death was coming for her, she knew this. How would she face the ancestors in the Pyramid if she sat there and watched this treacherous dog kill her master? This would not do.

Summoning all the rage of her people, she stood, and calling upon the strength of her fallen warrior brothers, she charged the assassin before he could strike the sleeping Scion. The two of them crashed through the side of the tent, collapsing that quarter of it.

Moriv woke with a start as the tent came down around him. Instinctively, he grasped Shadow Stealer and rolled to his feet. Where was Junaria? Why had the tent fallen?

Chapter 3

The fog of sleep receded from his mind, and he heard the crashing of fist on flesh and saw the movement within the silks of the tent. Quickly, he drew his blade and slashed through the fabric to find the source of the commotion. Traversing the grasping shreds of the tent, he cut his way through just in time for the commotion to be over.

He sliced his way into a pocket of the fabric and found Junaria slumped over the body of a black man dressed in colorful silks. The man's eyes were wide open. and his face was frozen with fear and lack of air. As the light of the stars fell upon the scene, Junaria stirred.

Moriv did not know what to do or what to say. He prayed silently that Junaria was unharmed. As she turned in his direction, he knew that he had prayed to the ancients in vain. One dagger was deeply stuck in her chest, another to one side of her abdomen. In the darkness, he could see the black rivers of blood that ran out from under her armor. Moriv took a step towards her as she tried to stand. She collapsed before she stood, and he leapt forward to try and catch her as she fell. He was not as agile and quick as he should have been.

Panic took him as he lifted her head to face him. When she opened her eyes and smiled, it shocked him.

"You are unhurt, Master?" she asked, weakly.

Moriv nodded.

She smiled again and slowly blinked her eyes. "I knew he would send someone for you, Scion. It was my duty to protect you, and now my duty is complete."

Moriv could feel the sting of tears come to his eyes. He could not bear the thought of being alone here. She was more than just a slave to him; she was his lover, his guardian, his world.

Shadow of the Pyramid

"Do not cry, Master. Win. Fight Gorand in the morning and spill his blood for all of us. All of your people that died to bring you here. Kill him." Even at death's door she was stronger than him. With these final words, she surrendered her soul.

At first, Moriv was numb, then he felt a rage build within him. He clutched Junaria's body close to his and wept dark tears of anger. When his clothes were soaked in the blood of his protector, he stood up and looked over at the torches burning in the camp for the men of Broken.

A slight breeze washed over his body, and he could feel the warmth leave the sticky blood that covered him. His only thoughts were of murder. In his head, he turned over a dream that always led to his death. Over and over, he imagined storming into Gorand's camp and fighting his way through and plunging Shadow Stealer into the chest of his rival. Over and over, it ended with Gorand's guards driving their spears into every part of Moriv's body.

Silently, the whispering stone whispered. It reminded him of his purpose here, of his people, and of his place as Scion of the Pyramid. He was not just simply a man who had had a loss - he was the will of his people. Sacrificing his life for revenge, as did the Scion who first wielded Shadow Stealer, would only hurt their future. The whispers calmed the rage, but they did not put out the fire. That could only be quenched in blood.

Moriv did not clean up the bodies or fix the tent. Instead, he sat in the middle of the standing portion and meditated. His senses reached out to the world around him, and he let the time pass. It was almost as if he had the power to force time forward in this trance. In his mind he could see the first rays of morning rise over the horizon. He could hear the stirring of the people and smell the wafting aroma of their morning meals.

Chapter 3

The sun rose in the sky, and so too did the temperature of the rise. Hot and humid, the morning stretched into the midday, and that is when he came for Moriv, the man who worked for Darvin.

"Oi! Whut happened in here?" the man said, with obvious shock.

Moriv rose to his feet, and collected Shadow stealer from the ground as he did so. "Nothing," he responded as he walked out into the town.

"Aren't you gunna put on your armor?" the man asked, then realized that Moriv's clothes were soaked in blood. "Oi! Is that your blood?"

Moriv thought for a moment before he responded flatly, "Yes." This wasn't strictly true, but in his current state of mind it was the blood of his people, and therefore is was his blood. He intended that Gorand should repay in kind.

When Moriv got to the Theatre of Blood, he looked at the board. The very first fight listed was between him and Gorand. Their tiles had been painted red. Moriv could only presume that this signified the duel had been designated as a fight to the death. There was nothing to do now but wait, so wait he did.

Many of the people stared at Moriv as they passed, whispering about the blood which caked his clothes and was smeared across his skin. The Scion did not care. He stood silently, staring off into the arena, waiting for his chance to kill Gorand.

Finally, he heard the woman at the board call his name, and he stepped into the pit. Gorand, too, stepped in, and with a mocking sneer, he spit in Moriv's direction.

"Have a rough night?" he asked with a sinister tone.

Moriv didn't respond. His face had the emotion of a dead man. The empty stare of the Scion unnerved Gorand.

Shadow of the Pyramid

"Nothing to say, shattered one?" Gorand mocked.

Again, Moriv just stood there and stared. He held Shadow Stealer limply in his left hand, and had a dagger in his right. He just stood there, waiting.

For a moment, Gorand regretted sending that assassin after Moriv. This no longer seemed like a man he was facing in the arena, but some undead thing risen to exact revenge. He was not alone in sensing the pure malice that oozed from Moriv. The entire crowd whispered about the intense look that he gave Gorand. Rumors started flying about the blood that covered the armorless body of the Scion.

The betting circle came to life with people trying to change their bets. Some thought that Moriv had gone insane and would fall easily under the blades of a veteran like Gorand. Others realized that there was more than just a man standing in Moriv's skin. They could feel the electric vengeance that pulsed inside him. This commotion fell dead as the woman at the scoreboard called out, "To the death! Fight!"

Before she had finished speaking, Moriv started calmly walking toward Gorand, but Gorand waited. As the words bellowed across the crowd, he let out a roar and charged at Moriv. In one fluid motion, Moriv planted Shadow Stealer upwards through Gorand's gut. The Scion twisted and shook the blade, driving it deeper into the warrior of Onisvaal's body.

Gorand vomited blood and dropped his blades into the dust, then collapsed lifelessly as Moriv swiftly withdrew Shadow Stealer. The Scion flicked the blood off his obsidian blade and dispassionately grimaced at the lifeless body that lay at his feet.

The entire crowd was silent. They were shocked at the brutally swift death that had been brought to Gorand, who the day before had been a crowd favorite to win.

Chapter 3

"Who is next?" Moriv shouted to the entire crowd. "Who else will stand between me and the Tomb of the Betrayer?"

Again the crowd was silent. Even the mockery of the men of Broken had been hushed. No one dared say anything, lest they face the murderous end of Moriv's blade.

Then from the crowd came a voice. "I withdraw."

"Marks Haas has withdrawn!" the woman at the board shouted.

"I, too, withdraw," a woman's voice could be heard saying.

Then a man's voice said, "I also withdraw."

From the scoreboard, a man's voice rolled over the crowd. "Then it is decided. Our champion is Moriv, Scion of The Great Obsidian Pyramid."

From the crowd there came a mixture of cheers and jeers. Many people walked away in disgust. Darvin swelled with pride and greed that his champion had won the day. Moriv did not care at all. He had done what he had come here to do, and now only one thing mattered: getting inside the tomb.

Shadow of the Pyramid

CHAPTER 4

The next morning found Moriv travelling through the jungle with several black-robed members of the Eternal Well, and Darvin's crew. The greedy little gambler from Skullspill would not stop talking about how amazing Moriv had been the day before, and eventually Moriv just tuned him out.

Through the overgrown path that the jungle had tried to reclaim, they cut their way to the east and approached the edge of the The Deepening. The cliff that loomed overhead was so immense that it made the Great Pyramid of Shatter seem like a cozy cottage. Birds launched themselves from nests atop the cliffs and disappeared into misty clouds that hung in the air.

Deeper and deeper they went into that eastern pit where the trees turned darker, more twisted, and sinister. A mist clung to the branches and was torn open by the trespassers that sliced their way into this heart of darkness. To Moriv, it felt like the very jungle was watching him and cursing his passage. His mind turned to the curse he had put on his own people, even Junaria. Had she grown to doubt him in the end? No, he could not bring himself to even ask that question. She was the closest to love a man from Shatter could ask for. Duty, service, and safety. Was it all just duty to her? He would never know the answers.

Shadow of the Pyramid

After he had defeated Gorand, he asked Darvin to help him with Junaria's body. What Jarvin did not expect was that Moriv would set the entire camp ablaze. While the silk tent, brush, and the bodies of Junaria and the assassin burned, Moriv just stood there and watched. He ignored the cries of Darvin's men who contained the fire that this shattered madman had set in the middle of their little town. Moriv silenced them with a whisper. "What does it matter anyway. This place is temporary. Its purpose has come to an end."

As dusk came to the jungle, the Eternal Well brought their charges to a hollow in the wilderness. There, carved into the very side of the cliff, was an archway of stone. Around the archway were hundreds, if not thousands, of carvings, reaching in every direction as far as the eye could see. They depicted a fight between good and evil, dragons trying to obliterate the host of mankind, and one Dragon standing with the forces of humanity. Above, the battle seemed to rage even in the heavens, and towards the ground, the battle seem to burn even the underworld where the dead rose to fight against the unearthly terror of the dragons. The archway itself was enormous, standing tall enough for the very trees to walk through without bending over.

Once the group came to the threshold, the black-robed-men and women of the Eternal Well stopped. Darvin and his men continued to walk, not noticing that their guides had stopped walking. Moriv, on the other hand, noticed.

"Why do you stop?" he asked them.

The same woman who spoke to Moriv days ago, Ingri, stepped forward. "We do not enter this sacred place. We only watch to see what happens."

Moriv paused and brushed his black moustache with his fingertips. "What tends to happen?"

Chapter 4

"Nothing," she said.

"Nothing?"

She smiled warmly at Moriv. "No one has ever found a way into the tomb, save those who made it."

He turned and cast his curious gaze over the ominous archway and the carvings that were a declaration to the world of what kind of place this was. A chill ran up Moriv's spine, and the whispering stone began singing to him. "Do people ever die trying to get in?"

Ingri shook her head. "Not that I have seen, though they do say that even the attempt to get in can change a person forever."

Moriv chuckled. He had been changed by his journey here. Perhaps that is what the adage meant, but perhaps there was a more sinister meaning.

"What are we waiting for, Scion? Let us use your strength to open the way!" Darvin's thrill from the day before had not let loose its grip.

Dark eyes scanned the opening the tomb. The whispers in his mind were comforting to Moriv, but something about this place had the cold stillness of death about it. "Darvin, take your men and go home. I thank you for your support, but this is for me to do."

Darvin was visibly disappointed. "But Moriv! I helped you get here! Don't you see? Without me, you wouldn't be here now!"

"And I appreciate your help, friend. Your assistance will not be forgotten by me, or by the people of Shatter, but it is time for you to go." Moriv's voice had the calm chill of a teacher chiding an unruly child.

The air between them was filled with a disappointed silence, which Darvin broke with a few stammering attempts to say any words at all. He huffed and growled, groaned and grunted, then finally said, "C'mon boys. We know when we aren't wanted."

"Thank you, Darvin. I am ever in your debt." Moriv bowed to Darvin as he passed.

The swindler from Skullspill grumbled something about repayment of debts as he vanished back into the jungle.

The Scion thought about asking Ingri and her company to leave, but he felt that would be a trickier conversation. Something about them said that they were there to stay, and Moriv was not interested in a verbal competition he could not win, so instead he planted his backside on the jungle floor and stared at the challenge before him. He had not even passed the threshold, as he did not know if that would simply prevent him from succeeding at this puzzle.

For a great long time he stared at that gate and the carvings around it. The Eternal Well lit torches around the hollow so that they would not be alone there in the dark. These torches would flicker in a non-existent breeze, and their color would sometimes change from the normal warm glow of flames to a hissing twist of purple fire, then before Moriv could even blink, the flames would return to their previous state. The Scion started to believe he was caught in some nightmare. Nothing felt right about this place, and he was unsure what to do.

Moriv fell asleep for a time, there in the hollow. His dreams were empty and black, and when he awoke, it felt like days had passed, but Ingri assured him that he had only nodded off for a few hours.

"Does it always go like this?" Moriv asked.

Ingri giggled, "No, Scion. Most who come here are so filled with their own glory that they do not even stop to see the great mural upon the wall. And when they find that there is no door for them to pull open with their mighty arms, they grow fiercely disappointed."

Chapter 4

Moriv wasn't disappointed. He was just hesitant to make a move without knowing what the rules of this puzzle were. He stood and brushed the earth from his body. When he looked at the side of the archway again, he saw a triangle, and at that very moment, the whispering stone sang to him with such excitement, he knew he must be on to something.

Closer he came to the stone wall, and found that this triangle was an icon depicting the Great Pyramid. Robed figures marched along each side the Pyramid, and they called down the might of the heavens against a dragonic foe. The moment that was trapped in stone before him showed that the battle was not going well for his people, yet they fought this draconic tyrant with all their combined strength.

Near to where Moriv stood, he also saw the tears of women that the carving transitioned into a river that fed the underworld. The moon hovered off to one side, and there were the souls of the dead who were being swept away into the moon as if it had the irresistible draw of a drain in the bottom of a basin. The souls silently screamed in horror as they were collected by another draconic demon that was the moon's master.

It was in these tears that Moriv found something interesting. A few of these tears were not the sandy brown stone of the cliffside. They were black stone, inlaid into the very sculpture. He looked closer and found that each was wrapped in edging of silverwork. Near these three black tears, there was a fourth hole, for a tear not yet placed.

Before the whispering could even flood into his mind, he was already scooping the stone out from around his neck. He held it near the hole and compared its size. Finding the stone to be a

Shadow of the Pyramid

perfect match, he broke the silver chain that held it close to him, and with a defiant glance at the terrible silvery moon that hung above him, he placed the stone within the hole, completing the mural.

A gasp and some whispering came from the members of the Eternal Well, but Moriv ignored them. Instead, he looked into the darkness beyond the archway and wondered.

"What secrets do you hide, friend?" he whispered aloud, and stepped beyond the threshold.

The pathway was dark and felt very open, the way the entrance to the Pyramid felt, only even larger. There was a constant cold breeze brushed against Moriv's face as he slowly stepped forward. Before him was nothing, only the darkness of the void. Each step called for more bravery than the last. Fear seeped into Moriv's mind, and he kept imagining a pit that he would never see coming, but step after step he found no such trap.

When his doubt paralyzed his legs, and his will begged him to go no further, he looked over his shoulder. Behind him, he saw the massive archway with hard edges of light from the flickering torches. There was no perceivable stone passageway around him. It was as if the archway had been carved into the blackness of a starless night. Standing there in the opening were the black-robed figures of the Eternal Well, spanning the threshold. Their poses seemed to indicate that they were in prayer, but all were different, some with their faces to the sky and arms outstretched, others with heads bowed in reverence. Whatever their manner of worship, they all did so upon their feet. Moriv found this curious, and he had the sinking feeling that they would not let him leave this dark tunnel, so he turned and pressed onward.

Chapter 4

With a few more steps, he could feel mist upon his face, and the air was now both cold and damp. Since his eyes were no use to him, Moriv closed their lids and continued to walk, shoving his fear and doubt away. There was no turning back.

"You can open your eyes, son," an aged voice spoke softly.

Moriv stopped walking forward. He realized that with the stone placed into the side of the outer wall of the tomb, he no longer had the whispering guidance of his ancestors. He almost complied, but then realized this could be a test or a trap. Instead he called out, "Who is there?"

The silence in the room felt oppressive. Each moment seemed to stretch on forever. While waiting, Moriv realized that the breeze was gone, and he could no longer feel the mist. Through his eyelids, he could even detect some faint blue light. He nearly sucumbed to the temptation to open his eyes, but stood still and silent.

"I... I am trapped in this place. Alone and cold. I was once a man, like you, but no longer," the voice finally said. "Open your eyes and entreat with me, son."

The voice was warm and old enough to cause Moriv worry. He was not sure how to act, or if the voice's master was his friend or foe. There was nothing else for it, however; eventually Moriv would have to open his eyes, and then was as good a time as any.

The room was smaller than Moriv had expected, though if he had been asked, he would have said did not know what to expect. The carved walls were smooth, with superior craftsmanship, and the four square pillars that held aloft the unseen roof were emblazoned with the images of people. These carvings were larger than life and depicted faces Moriv did not know and clothing he did not recognize, save one pillar. Upon one of its faces there was an image

Shadow of the Pyramid

of the Princes of Onisvaal, or at least one man who looked like all seven. His clothing and jewelry was dripping with elegance, and his face screamed of pride and greed. It could be no other than them.

He saw another man, clad in armor from neck to toe. His face was commanding and ferocious, and his armor was carved with images of macabre violation of the dead. Another man was a regal and heroic king, with a crown made of raven's wings. Among all these he also found a man who looked like a simple farmer, with only scraps of mismatched fabric has his clothes. One final image did he see before his investigation was disturbed: a woman, impossibly tall, with features that were almost alien. Her hair seemed alive around her, and her face was serene and beautiful. Even this carving of her was so charming that Moriv nearly fell in love with it at first glance.

"Who are all these faces, you might ask," the old voice said softly. "I do not know their names, nor do I know if they are even still alive in the world outside. So please, do not ask."

Moriv looked for the source of the voice, but found no one stirring there in the dim blue light. Stepping deeper into the space before him, Moriv saw what looked like a throne carved into the back wall, but a throne with empty shackles and chains attached. This was no place to hold court; it was a prison.

"This place once held The Betrayer, did it not?" Moriv asked the emptiness of the room.

"Aye. That it did, son. That it did."

Moriv's patience was waning. This place was a puzzle he did not care to solve. His purpose was singular, and he meant to go directly onward. "Where is the Thorn of Eternity?"

Chapter 4

The old voice laughed and coughed, "People who come looking for powerful things are often fools. What purpose do you have for such a terrible thing, son? Looking to be a hero? Want to rid the world of evils older than time itself? What is it you want?"

Images of Junaria flooded Moriv's mind. He wanted her. More than anything he wanted her to be there with him, and alive. His jaw clenched and his fingers curled into involuntary fists. "I want what the ancients have sent me here for. The dagger."

"The ancients? My my. You are from Dius, aren't you? Of course, that would explain your entrance and your arrogance," the old man's voice laughed again, giving way to a deathly cough. "The masters of the Mari'Andi have never been known for subtlety when they are desperate. So they must be very desperate indeed."

Moriv's face flashed with rage. "What do you know of desperation, hidden one? Come out and show us who you are!"

"Would that I could, son. But I am long since dead, and trapped in this place. Perhaps you can do us a favor, and in exchange we can show you this dagger you seek."

Doing dealings with spirits of the dead was not exactly Moriv's area of expertise, though he would perhaps argue that he had found himself here at the will of hundreds of dead ancestors. Somehow he felt oddly comfortable with the proposal, even if he should not have. "First, tell me who you were in life."

The old voice sighed, "Very well, son. In an age long past, I was a wizard. My home was a tower, far to the west of this place. My murder came at the hands of one of those who build this place and imprisoned the one you call The Betrayer."

Moriv was stunned, "You were a wizard of the Great Tower?"

Shadow of the Pyramid

"Indeed." The old voice sounded tired. "I know the Mari'Andi had no love for those of us who lived at the tower, but I am too tired for games and tricks, child. Do we have a deal?"

Moriv nodded slowly and said, "I accept your deal, wizard. Now where is the Thorn?"

A door popped open near the throne in the back of the hall, and Moriv went to open it further. The massive stone took all his strength to slide aside, and the Scion had to rest several times while trying to pull and push it open. Eventually the space was wide enough for him to slip through.

The blue light from the chamber followed him through the crack of the door, and seemed to walk ahead of him in the tunnel that descended before him.

"Come now, child. The thing you seek is this way."

Moriv followed the blue glow down the twisting path deeper into the earth. The smell of ash and dust grew stronger with each step into the depths. Finally they came to another chamber. This one looked as if it had been carved from the rock by persistent and desperate claws. Roots from unseen trees and plants invaded from the ceiling and gave more texture to the mix of earth and stone that made up the walls. The ground was uneven and dark. In the center of the room was a massive stone that looked like a slab to display a corpse, but smaller. The area around this flat rectangle of stone was burnt black and covered in soot. One set of footprints could be seen in the ashes, and they led from the stone outwards to the steps.

"What is this place, wizard?" Moriv tried to hide the nervousness in his voice.

"It is the anvil where the last voice of dark things was forged."

Chapter 4

Moriv stepped into the room and immediately was swept away in the undertow of rage and sorrow that filled this place. Guilt and fear was so thick in the air that he could barely breathe.

"Steady on, child. Do not lose your way in this place, or the forge will claim your very soul. This anger, guilt, and sorrow was not meant for you. Let it go."

Moriv tried to do as the voice asked, but his heart collapsed under the weight of Junaria's memory. He should have woken sooner. The assassin should not have been able to kill Junaria. She was a titan, an indestructible mountain. The Pyramid should have chosen her to be the Scion, not him. Who was he to the world?

"Child of the Pyramid. Do not give up your hope!" the old voice commanded, and the light in the room grew brighter than daylight. "Stand upon your feet and claim that which is yours, oh lord of terror!"

The light pushed away the fog of fear and doubt, and when Moriv opened his eyes, he found himself curled in a ball upon the floor. Everywhere he looked he saw nothing staring back at him, but he felt the malice of the very room trying to crush his soul.

"There, upon the anvil. Take up the dagger and the bowl. Carry them to the surface and scatter the ashes. NOW!"

Whispering began seeping into Moriv's mind and the blue light of his unseen ally began to dim. Like a man possessed, Moriv lunged for the dagger that sat within a cradle on the rectangular stone, and try as he might, he could not pull it from its rest.

Panic took root, and Moriv's eyes looked to the exit of the chamber. It was so far away, and the shadows were so very dark. How would he escape?

"I am that which steals the shadow's ire," a whisper cut through the rest in his mind.

Shadow of the Pyramid

Shocked, Moriv looked around for the source of the whisper and found he was still alone, the blue glow dimming further with every moment.

"Who was that?" Moriv called to the darkness.

"I am that which steals the shadow's ire," the whisper repeated.

Inspiration struck Moriv like lightning, and he swiftly drew Shadow Stealer from his belt. Immediately the air around the blade began to vibrate, twist, and tear the very shadows around it. The Scion knew then what he had to do. Holding the blade like those acolytes in the Pyramid that cleansed his soul with incense, he waved Shadow Stealer around the dagger and the bowl. The shadows that held the dagger in place were shredded away and began writhing at the obsidian shard in his hand.

With one quick scoop, he picked up the dagger with his left hand. His eyes darted to the bowl filled with ashes and then back to his hands, both filled. Before he could think of another plan, he placed Shadow Stealer in the cradle where he had stolen the dagger and quickly snatched the bowl from the stone surface. Without a second thought, he ran for the passage that would lead him from that deep dark, place. The blue light followed nigh upon, and from behind him, he could hear the sizzling howl of crackling air. Moriv did not stop to see what that was.

The Scion ran up the carved passageway, stumbling twice as he tripped over rocks and roots on the way up. When he entered the smoothly crafted room, he did not stop, but headed directly for the dark passage that carried him within, and left.

Somewhere in the dark passage, Moriv slipped the dagger into his belt, behind his back. Later he would assume that he did so to hide it from whomever might meet him at the entrance, but he could never be quite sure.

Chapter 4

As he guessed, the Eternal Well was still outside when he came to the archway. Stepping out of the dark passage, he pushed through them as he broke the threshold.

With a mixture of joy and surprise, Ingri said, "Scion! You have returned! What did you find inside?"

Moriv held out the dark metal bowl filled with but a few pinches of ashes and said, "This. I found this." He was out of breath.

Without thinking about it, Moriv handed Ingri the bowl, and she took it over to the other black-robed men and women.

Tired from his ordeal, Moriv nearly collapsed to the jungle floor. His mind wandered to the voice from inside the tomb. He could not help but fear that he had let some imprisoned horror escape that terrible place. It was too late for worry now, he supposed.

As Moriv rested, Ingri approached and said, "Thank you for giving us the ashes. We will take care of them from here. Do you need escort back to the camp?"

"No," Moriv responded. "I will find my own way from here."

Exactly where he would go, he was not sure. He knew only what the ancestors had told him: the dagger would lead him to the blade of the Betrayer, and to whomever wielded it.

After Ingri and the Eternal Well had left, Moriv sat alone in the moonlight. He pulled the dagger out from his belt and turned it over and over in his hands. It was a sinister looking blade with a very sharp point. In form it almost looked like the tusk or tooth from some animal, but it was entirely pitch black. The handle was a fragment of an animal's antler wrapped in sinewy red leather.

"Thorn of Eternity?" he asked the dagger. "Seems like an odd name for something so simple. Why so much trouble for such a little thing?"

Shadow of the Pyramid

Moriv stood and looked back into the dark archway of the tomb. His ordeal seemed almost silly now. He was the Scion of the Great Obsidian Pyramid, on an important mission. It was embarrassing that he was frightened of an empty room.

"What is done is done," he said to no one in particular and then started to walk.

After several days spent sleeping and nights spent hunting and avoiding the dangers of the jungle, he found himself climbing out of The Deepening alone. At the top, he saw an expanse of sand that quickly turned into grassland. He was on the north side of the chasm. Going south would just take him back to Shatter, and his mission was not done. In that moment he decided where to go next.

Moriv took a deep breath and brushed his moustache out to the sides of his mouth. "Let the ancestors guide my path," he said to the wind, and took a step towards the great city of Flay.

Made in the USA
Charleston, SC
30 August 2014